SAMMAEL'S WINGS

HILTON PASHLEY

Andersen Press

First published in 2015 by
Andersen Press
20 Vauxhall Bridge Road
London SW1V 2SA
www.andersenpress.co.uk

2 4 6 8 10 9 7 5 3 1

British Library Cataloguing in Publication Data available.

ISBN 978 1 78344 325 3

Typeset in Goudy by Palimpsest Book Production Limited,
Falkirk, Stirlingshire

Printed and bound by CPI Group (UK) Ltd, Croydon, CR0 4YY

For Aimee and Eleanor

'God will not look you over for medals, degrees or diplomas,
but for scars.'
Elbert Hubbard

'Know ye not that we shall judge the angels?'
Corinthians 6:3

CONTENTS

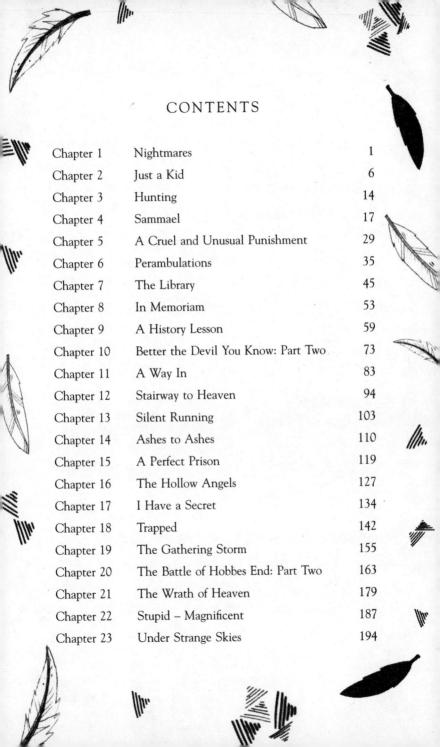

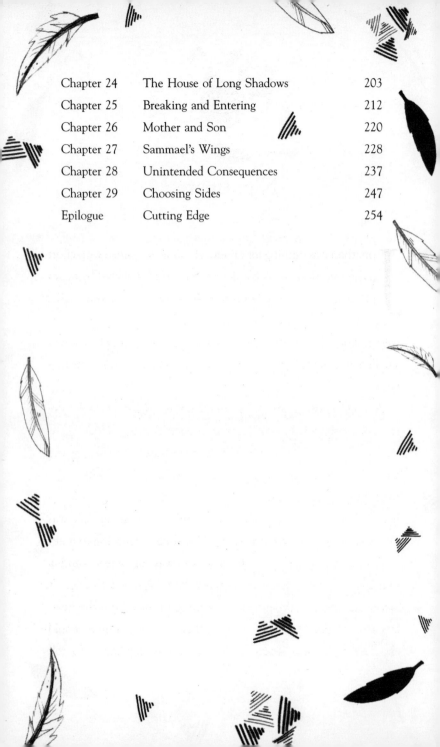

Nightmares

J onathan was running for his life. His lungs screamed with effort as he tore along a marble-floored boulevard, buffeted by waves of heat from the burning buildings on either side. A thick, greasy smoke hugged the ground, and an unfamiliar stench filled his nostrils as he gasped for breath. He'd never smelled it before, but somehow he knew what it was: burning flesh.

A huge crash to his left signalled the collapse of a house; red-hot masonry and smouldering wooden beams exploded into the street in front of him, carpeting the marble with glowing cinders. Knowing that to stand still for too long would be to die, Jonathan vaulted over the obstruction and ignored the pain as his clothes began to scorch. The marble beneath his feet was now so hot he could feel the soles of his shoes beginning to melt.

An agonised cry came from a doorway up ahead, and a humanoid figure wreathed in orange flame lurched through it before slumping to the ground. Shielding his face from the heat, Jonathan skidded to a halt to see if there was anything he could do. The figure was so badly burned it was impossible to tell whether it was male or female, and flames still danced across the blackened skin. The awful wreckage of the figure's face was turned towards Jonathan, and it seemed that life had mercifully fled under the weight of such terrible suffering.

Worse still, from the figure's back protruded two blackened, ragged clumps. Jonathan looked closer – squinting through the heat haze – and saw that there were white patches untouched by flame. He reached out a trembling hand and brushed one of the patches with his fingertips; it was covered with . . . feathers. Jonathan felt tears begin to sting the corners of his eyes, but the liquid evaporated in the heat before it had time to run down his face.

'This was an angel,' he said to himself, horrified.

A vicious crackling erupted from behind him, and he turned to see a wall of fire leap across the boulevard: a wall which began moving rapidly forward. With his throat too dry to scream and his clothes beginning to smoulder, Jonathan dragged himself away from the dead angel and ran. The skin of his feet began to blister along with that of his hands and face, and the din behind him grew louder and closer. Breathing was almost impossible as the superheated air seared the inside of his lungs with every painful gasp.

He glanced over his shoulder and his eyes widened in terror as he saw that the wall of fire was gaining on him. He willed his wings to manifest themselves, desperately wanting to hear the joyful song of power that accompanied those serrated purple ribbons. With his wings outspread and the mathematics of creation itself coursing through his veins, he could outrun the inferno and escape. But nothing happened. His wings remained silent: no song, no power, no way out.

'*No!*' Jonathan cried as he forced the tortured muscles of his legs to keep moving. He had fought the archdemon Belial and won; he didn't deserve to die in agony, reduced to a blackened corpse like that poor angel.

Half-blind in the writhing smoke, Jonathan stepped on something that gave way with a crack and sent him sprawling into what felt like a pile of kindling. He thrust out his right hand to break his fall and felt it jam into something dry and hard. He pulled his arm back and came face to face with a jawless skull, his fingers buried deep in the eye sockets. With a cry, Jonathan flung the awful thing away and struggled to his feet. Looking about him he could see what had tripped him up – bones. He was knee-deep in a mountain of humanoid bones: skulls, femurs, fingers, and scapulae, some of which were very small, like those of children.

Utterly exhausted and reeling with shock, Jonathan sank to his knees and bowed his head as the inferno raced towards him, its hungry light reflecting on the polished marble. The heat grew in intensity, and Jonathan gritted his teeth as his jacket began to burn. The roar of the flames filled his head as he shut his eyes and prepared to die.

Without warning the heat and light suddenly vanished. Blessed darkness and cold air played around Jonathan's face, soothing his burns. He slowly opened his eyes, wondering why he wasn't dead. The bones were still there, but the space around him was dark, chill and silent, like an ash-filled mortuary.

'Look at me,' said a soft, youthful voice from directly behind him.

Jonathan almost jumped out of his skin. He wanted to see who had spoken but dare not move; it was sure to be yet more horror for him to endure.

'Look at me,' the voice said again. 'Turn your head and look at me.'

Terrified of what he might see but desperate to find some comfort in this dire place, Jonathan turned round. He was stunned to see a young boy of similar age and height to himself, wearing simple leather sandals and a white, short-sleeved tunic, belted at the waist. The boy's long, fair hair was pulled back and tied loosely with a gold silk cord, and from his shoulders grew a pair of wings that arced up above his head, white-feathered and glorious.

'The fire,' Jonathan croaked. 'How did you . . . ?'

'There's no need to be afraid,' said the angel. 'I've been waiting for you. I have someone you've been looking for.'

The angel reached out a hand, and from the swirling smoke emerged the tall figure of a man. He wore a similar tunic to that of the boy, but it was stained by splotches of dried blood.

Jonathan shifted his gaze from the tunic to the man's face. His father's eyes stared back at him.

'Dad . . . ?' gasped Jonathan. 'Dad, I've found you!'

'My son,' replied Darriel, his face pale and sad. 'I need your help. I'm wounded, see?' He turned and showed Jonathan the torn and ragged remains of what had once been two mighty wings. 'This is what Belial and the Corvidae did before leaving me for dead on the steps of Heaven. Please help me, my son.'

'We both need you,' begged the boy angel, his handsome face as smooth as polished alabaster.

Jonathan made to stand up, but stopped short when he heard a guttural moan from close by. He looked to his left and saw the horrifically burned body of an adult angel, clawing his agonised way towards him across the bone-strewn ground. From his face, a pair of blazing blue eyes fixed their gaze upon him.

'Help us!' repeated Darriel, his voice strangely flat and unemotional.

The burned angel drew level with Jonathan and reached out to grab his ankle. Frozen to the spot in utter terror, Jonathan could only watch as the angel opened his blackened mouth to speak. 'No! Don't. Don't help. Stay awaaaaaay!' The angel pulled himself even closer, his eyes boring into Jonathan's. 'STAY AWAAAAAAY!' To hammer the point home, the angel's hand suddenly burst into flame, burning right through Jonathan's jeans and searing his skin.

It was only then that Jonathan finally began to scream.

Just a Kid

Elgar was sound asleep and dreaming happily. He was just about to pounce on a giant kipper he'd been stalking when a scream shattered his slumber.

'What the hell was that?' he spluttered, only to fall off the draining board where he'd been curled up and land in an ungainly heap in his basket.

Halcyon Grimm – who was asleep at the kitchen table with a copy of *The Times* steepled across his face – bolted upright in surprise, knocking over a mug and spilling cold tea everywhere. He blinked and looked at Elgar. 'Was that Jonathan?' he asked the cat.

'Sounded like it,' replied Elgar. Without delay they ran from the kitchen and up the stairs, meeting Ignatius on the landing. The vicar of Hobbes End was barefoot, wearing a dressing gown, and his hair was sticking up at all angles.

'Is Jonathan all right?' asked Grimm.

'I don't know,' said Ignatius. 'Come on, let's see what's wrong.' He knocked gently on Jonathan's bedroom door, but when he didn't receive an answer he opened it regardless. 'Jonathan?' he said softly, poking his head round the door to see the boy sitting on his bed in a tangle of sweat-drenched sheets, hugging his knees to his chest.

Jonathan looked at Ignatius with haunted, dark-rimmed eyes. 'I had a nightmare,' he said.

'It sounded like a whopper,' said Elgar, padding into the room and jumping onto the bed. 'I haven't heard a scream like that since my aunt Agatha accidentally ate her own arm.'

Despite himself Jonathan smiled at the cat. 'How is that even possible?'

'Too much daytime television,' replied Elgar. 'Anyhow, what's got you all screamy?'

Jonathan rested his head on his knees for a moment as he took a deep breath. He could see his chest wall pulsing in time with his runaway heart. 'I was stuck somewhere and everything was burning. It was so hot and I could barely breathe . . . and there was this *smell*.'

'What kind of smell?' asked Grimm.

Jonathan shuddered and closed his eyes. 'Burning people,' he whispered.

'So, not one of those dreams where you end up taking an exam wearing just a pair of hiking boots?' said Elgar.

Jonathan shook his head and ruffled the cat's fur. 'I wish.'

'There's something else, isn't there?' asked Ignatius, his face grave. 'Just like me, you have a bond with Hobbes End; this village has a soul, remember? It can feel your distress, as can I.'

Jonathan nodded and looked at the vicar. 'I saw a burning

angel, and then all these bones – a mountain of them. Just when I thought I was going to burn too, everything stopped and a boy angel spoke to me.'

'A boy angel?'

'Yeah,' said Jonathan. 'He said he'd been waiting for me and that he had someone I'd been looking for.' He paused, tears welling up.

'It's all right,' Ignatius reassured him.

'But it's not,' said Jonathan. 'My dad was there too. He looked at me and he was so sad. He was really hurt and he begged me to help him. He's been missing for weeks now and I'm still no closer to finding him. Is he calling out to me somehow from wherever he is? D'you think he's waiting for me to rescue him?'

Ignatius sighed and gently patted Jonathan on the shoulder. 'I don't know, lad,' he said.

'Dad showed me what the Corvidae had done to him, Ignatius. Those monsters tore his wings off and left him to die on the steps of Heaven. And . . . isn't Heaven sealed from the inside? Nobody has gone in or out for decades . . .'

Ignatius nodded. 'Yes. Gabriel could never understand why his brother Raphael did that. All right, he is the eldest archangel, and he is in charge of Heaven, but even if he is as . . . unstable as Gabriel feared, surely he would not let your father suffer. Somebody inside Heaven would open the gates.'

'I don't know,' said Jonathan. 'We were told that Raphael had gone insane. Would a mad angel care about helping my dad?'

'Yes, but we were told that by Belial: a vicious, manipulative archdemon,' said Ignatius. 'He wanted to use you as a weapon to conquer his enemies and he tore your family apart in the process. You sent him screaming back to Hell, remember, so don't let his lies upset you. And as for the demons of the Corvidae, well, we know what happened to them. Grimm and I made sure that Rook, Raven and Crow will never hurt another soul. We have their bowler hats to prove it.'

'Yeah,' nodded Jonathan. 'I'm glad you killed them. They were monsters.'

'That they were, Jonny,' said Elgar. 'They hurt my family too, remember? I'm stuck in this fetching feline body because of Belial's curse. Sometimes even I forget that I'm actually a demon boy.'

'I know, cat,' said Jonathan, gently ruffling the fur on his friend's head.

'We make a right pair,' said Elgar. 'Who would think you're actually half-angel, half-demon, and all badass when you need to be?'

Jonathan couldn't help but smile at his friend.

'Now that's better,' said Elgar, playfully butting Jonathan's shin.

'Ow!' cried Jonathan, snatching his leg away from the cat.

'What?' asked Elgar. 'I didn't bite you or anything!'

'No, it's not that,' said Jonathan, hurriedly pulling the sheets away and swinging his legs to the side of the bed where he could see them clearly. 'Oh God, look!'

Ignatius, Grimm and Elgar all craned to see what Jonathan

was pointing at. There at the bottom of his left leg, just above the ankle, was a livid burn. The skin was blistered, red and weeping, but that wasn't the worst of it.

'Is it just my tired old eyes, or does that burn look like it's in the shape of a *hand*?' asked Grimm. 'Sit there while I go and get my bag; that burn needs dressing.'

Jonathan nodded, but inside he felt empty; the injury confirmed that his nightmare was no mere bad dream.

Once Grimm had finished applying cream and bandages, he brought Jonathan a mug of steaming hot chocolate and left him alone with Ignatius and Elgar.

'What should I do?' Jonathan asked.

Ignatius paused and sucked on his unlit pipe. 'I think you should start by looking for your father at his last known location.'

'The steps of Heaven? And how do I get there?' asked Jonathan. 'Grandfather – Gabriel – told me that there was a path between Hell and the steps of Heaven; and the Corvidae used it when they left Dad there. But I don't know where the entrance is.'

'And you can't exactly wander around Hell looking for it,' said Ignatius, taking off his glasses to rub his tired eyes.

Jonathan shook his head.

'What about Gabriel's Clock?' suggested Ignatius, gesturing to the ordinary-looking wristwatch that sat on Jonathan's bedside table. 'Your grandfather built it so that his magnificent knowledge wouldn't be lost. You were wearing it when he died, so all that knowledge rests inside you now. And let's not forget that somehow it's supposed to be able to open a secret door into Gabriel's old workshop in Heaven.'

'Yeah, I know,' said Jonathan. 'If I could get into Heaven itself, then I could look for Dad there too, find out if someone took him in and has been caring for him, but I have no idea how to open that secret door. The answer is somewhere inside my head but I don't know how to find it. It's like . . . it's like walking into a huge room crammed with shelves of books, but there are no titles on the spines and no filing system. I *know* so much now, but I don't *understand* any of it! I'm just so tired.'

'I know,' said Ignatius. 'But it's only been a week since I watched you – a twelve-year-old boy who didn't know who or what he really was until just recently – go toe-to-toe with an archdemon and win, saving us all. Go easy on yourself, lad; the injuries you received in your fight with Belial have only just begun to heal.' He paused. 'If David had grown up to be like you, I would have been very proud indeed.'

Jonathan looked at Ignatius and smiled. He knew what a huge compliment he had just received from the deeply private cleric. Ignatius rarely spoke about the deaths of his wife and son.

'I'm so worried about Mum too,' sighed Jonathan, stroking the fur on Elgar's back for comfort. 'I don't know what's happened to her, either. She's somewhere in Hell because she tried to go and get help from Lucifer but she's lost – and it's only because she wanted to save me. We may have beaten Belial, but what use is all this power I've been given if I can't even help my parents? My mum is missing, and my dad is probably dying on the steps of Heaven; it doesn't feel like much of a victory.'

'You didn't cause any of this, Jonathan,' said Ignatius. 'Your parents did their best to keep you safe and you mustn't blame yourself for it. A parent will do anything to protect their child, remember that.'

Jonathan nodded. He knew the truth of what Ignatius was saying, but the ache of his parents' absence was with him all the time – and it was getting worse.

'It'll be a new day soon,' said Ignatius. 'Who knows where help may come from? I know this nightmare has upset you and there's probably more to it than meets the eye, but for now you need to sleep. Don't forget that we have the memorial service for Gabriel tomorrow evening.'

Jonathan settled back into his pillows, his eyes once again filling with tears. 'I miss my grandfather as well.'

Ignatius nodded, the sadness on his face mirroring that of Jonathan's. 'Me too,' he said. 'Now, how about I read to you for a bit; keep the night terrors away.'

Jonathan closed his eyes, lulled by the soft sound of Ignatius's voice as it told him the story of a fictional young boy, battling against the forces of darkness.

Grimm looked up from the sink where he was washing his hands. 'They all right?' he asked Elgar.

'I think so,' replied the cat as he padded into the kitchen. 'Ignatius is reading to Jonathan from *Henry Cobbler and the Teapot of Doom*, or something. Never understood the attraction of kids' fantasy books myself.'

'But you're just a kid too,' said Grimm.

'*Just* a kid, eh?' said Elgar, raising an eyebrow.

'That's not what I meant and you know it,' said Grimm. 'We're not expecting you or Jonathan – or Cay – to start taking on the responsibilities of an adult. It's not fair on any of you; nobody should be forced to grow up too fast.'

'Well, I s'pose not,' said Elgar. 'Still, cometh the hour, cometh the cat and all that. Can I have a kipper?'

Grimm chuckled to himself and opened the fridge.

Hunting

It was a night for dreams in Hobbes End. Across the green from the vicarage, Jonathan's best friend Cay lay on her bed asleep. Beneath closed lids her eyes flicked to and fro with alarming rapidity. Her limbs twitched, and she raised her nose to sniff the stuffy, late-summer air of her bedroom. Lost inside her own reality, Cay was a wolf, and she was hunting.

The forest about her was familiar and comforting. She had known it all her life, but here in the night as she ran along hidden paths and game trails, she was discovering a new face to nature. It didn't matter that it was dark; her lupine eyes sucked in every ray of moonlight and lit up her surroundings. Every leaf, every frond of bracken, every animal was rimmed with a shining silver halo.

And it wasn't just her sight; her sense of smell was so acute it was almost overwhelming. The damp floor of the forest exhaled and told her everything she needed to know. Dropping her head she quickened her pace, putting one paw in front of another with increasing speed until she was almost flying through the trees. Her heart beat strongly in her chest, and she exulted in the feeling of being so free.

She could sense water up ahead, and within seconds she had burst from the forest and was hurtling round the lake, ducking beneath the hanging sheets of weeping willow as she ran. She was upon the rabbit before it knew she was there. Without hesitation she grabbed the back of its neck with her jaws and ended the unfortunate creature's life with a single bite. There was an odd taste in her mouth, warm and metallic, but not unpleasant. She dropped her prize and looked down at the mangled animal lying between her paws; the life leaking from it had its own special halo. Suddenly Cay felt incredibly sad. She pushed at the rabbit with her muzzle but it remained still, its head twisted at an odd angle and its eyes wide open.

I have killed, she thought.

Leaving her prey, she padded to the edge of the lake and washed her muzzle in the cold water, removing all traces of the kill from her mouth. Raising her head, she could see the almost-full moon hanging in a cloudless sky. She found its light comforting, as if it was shining just for her. Opening her jaws, she called out to the moon as loudly as she could, her howl bouncing across the surface of the lake and fading into the forest. 'I am here,' she called. 'I am here.'

Kenneth and Joanne Forrester sat next to Cay's bed and watched her as she dreamed. Joanne – her face betraying her concern – signed to her husband.

'Yes, love,' he replied in sign language. 'It seems that Cay will share my burden after all. Her body is changing just as mine did at her age. She'll be able to transform into a wolf at will. I'll teach her all I can and she won't suffer the way I did. She will never think of herself as a monster. She'll be a werewolf and proud of it.'

Kenneth reached out and squeezed his wife's hand as his eyes filled up with tears.

Joanne returned the squeeze before cupping his bearded face and kissing him tenderly on the cheek. She signed again.

Kenneth nodded in agreement. 'I know it's difficult to watch,' he said. 'But she is not suffering – she is . . . becoming. She will be loved no matter what; there is nothing to be afraid of.' Giving Joanne a reassuring smile, he returned to gently mopping his daughter's forehead with a cold flannel.

Sammael

'**M**orning!' Cay called out as she stuck her head round the open back door of the vicarage. She peered into the kitchen to spy Jonathan, Elgar, Ignatius and Grimm sitting at the table, having tea and toast.

'Morning,' came the chorused reply. Grimm pushed out a spare chair for Cay without taking his eyes from the sports page of *The Times*.

'What's so interesting?' she asked him.

'Cricket,' he replied. 'Specifically, the performance of the English cricket team against Australia. Note that I put particular emphasis on the word *performance*.'

'Bet they'd play better if you were on the team,' said Cay.

'Damn right,' growled Grimm.

'If Grimm was on the team he could play the Aussies on his own,' said Elgar. 'The rest of them could sit in the pavilion, eat cucumber sandwiches and watch in awe. You are talking about the man who – while using a cricket bat named Isobel – killed both Rook and Crow of the Corvidae, nasty demons both, and gave the archdemon Belial a very good thrashing.'

'It was a team effort, but thank you for your vote of confidence,' chuckled Grimm.

'You're quiet,' Cay said to Jonathan, who was staring into his tea and frowning.

'Sorry,' he said. 'I had an awful nightmare last night and my head feels a bit fuzzy.'

'I had a strange dream too,' she said.

Jonathan waited for her to continue, but when Cay asked if she could have a mug of tea it was obvious that she didn't want to discuss it.

'What was your nightmare about?' she asked instead.

'It was horrible,' Jonathan said. 'I was running along this—'

He was interrupted when a double rap on the front door echoed along the vicarage hallway.

'That's . . . odd,' said Ignatius.

'What is?' said Jonathan. 'It's probably the postman or something.'

'No, it's not the postman, it's Hobbes End; the village feels as though it's holding its breath.'

Jonathan concentrated on his ever-deepening link with the village. It was still in its infancy, but every day he felt more connected to Hobbes End and its moods. Some days it was happy; on others it could be sad, playful, capricious or silly – just like a person. Today, the village was unusually quiet, but it was a quiet that comes from deliberately trying to hide something. It couldn't be anything bad – Gabriel had created the village as a sanctuary and no evil could cross its borders without catching fire – so what could it be?

There was another double rap on the front door – harder this time – as though patience was wearing thin.

'*Fine*,' moaned Elgar, jumping down from his chair and stretching. 'I'll get it then. My chilled morning vibe has been thoroughly dented by all this racket.' Stalking out of the kitchen, the cat padded silently along the hall towards the front door. He was almost there when he heard the squeak of the heavy knocker being raised yet again. 'Hang on, hang on, I'm coming!' he shouted. 'Just give me a minute to open the door, will you? I'm a cat, I don't have opposable thumbs.'

Reaching up, Elgar dug his claws into the decorative door handle and swung himself sideways, simultaneously pushing at the architrave with his back legs. The front door swung inward, and the cat dropped gracefully to the floor before he got squashed against the wall.

'What?' he growled, blinking at the figure standing in silhouette against the morning sun.

A cricket ball thudded onto the doormat in front of the cat. 'Is this yours?' asked a quiet, authoritative and unmistakably female voice.

'Um . . . no,' said Elgar, wondering who on earth the visitor was. 'But I know whose it is. Would you like to come in and return it?'

'Yes, I think I would,' said the figure, stepping forward into the shade of the hallway so Elgar could see her properly. He stared upward at a tall, slim woman, dressed in a full-length black coat. It flared out around her ankles, was cut in tightly at the waist and securely buttoned up to a high, almost clerical collar. She wore black leather gloves, black leather boots, and long hair the colour of morning frost was tied loosely at the nape of her neck with a simple black ribbon. She had an expressive, angular face, a wry mouth, firm chin and straight nose. It was her eyes that bothered Elgar – the irises kept slowly changing colour from silver to blue and back again. They spoke of great age and terrible sadness.

The woman coughed politely.

'Oh, sorry, just staring,' said a flummoxed Elgar. 'If you'd kindly follow me?'

Picking up the cricket ball with his mouth, he trotted down the hall, leaving the visitor to shut the front door behind her. Scurrying into the kitchen, Elgar bounded onto the table and dropped his prize into Grimm's mug of tea.

'A nice lady brought your ball back,' said the cat before jumping to the floor and curling up in his basket. Wide-eyed with curiosity, he peeped over the edge to see what happened next.

'Eh?' said Grimm, scowling at the dribble-covered ball that bobbed in his morning mug of freshly brewed Darjeeling.

Everyone stared at the open door to the hallway as an unfamiliar figure stepped into the kitchen.

'You may not have been expecting me,' said the woman, 'but I came anyway.' She stared intently at Ignatius before giving him a warm smile. 'You look so like your father,' she said.

Ignatius tried to speak, but all that came out was a strangled *glarp* sound.

'And you must be Halcyon,' she continued, shining her smile at the big man.

Grimm nodded dumbly, raising his mug of tea to his lips and banging himself on the nose with the cricket ball that still floated in it.

'I gather that's yours. It almost hit me on the head. Luckily I have very good reflexes.'

Grimm just stared at her in confusion.

'And you must be Cay,' said the woman. 'Dear child, your laughter is wonderful. I've been listening to it and it warms my heart.'

Cay sat open-mouthed, not knowing how to answer.

'And you,' said the woman, her piercing gaze fixed on Jonathan. 'You must be my great-nephew. You really do have your grandfather's eyes.'

Jonathan blinked in astonishment.

'Are you who I think you are?' croaked Ignatius, his unlit pipe dangling loosely from the corner of his mouth.

'That depends on who you think I am,' said the woman. She paused a moment before putting him out of his misery. 'I'm Sammael Morningstar, but you can call me Sam if you like.'

Ignatius's pipe fell with a plop into his mug. 'Oh, I've got to stop doing that,' he said.

Sammael waited for an invitation to join everyone at the table. Coming to his senses, Grimm scrambled to his feet, pulled out a chair and asked her if she would like some tea.

'That would be lovely,' said Sammael, watching Ignatius fish his dripping pipe from his mug.

'So you're Gabriel's sister . . . ?' said Jonathan.

Sammael nodded and smiled at him. 'Yes,' she said. 'But I'm not sure I deserve to be called that. I let my brother down when he needed me most, and I wasn't here to help him – or you – when Belial attacked. I felt Gabriel die, and at that moment I knew where I needed to be.'

'Where *were* you then?' asked Ignatius. 'We almost lost everything, and the price of victory was very high indeed.'

'I know,' said the angel. 'I didn't realise what was happening until it was too late. I have been away from Hobbes End for a very long time. Did Gabriel ever tell you about how we ended up here?'

'Yes,' said Jonathan. 'We had dinner in the vicarage soon after I arrived. He said that you were exiled from Heaven because of an accident which killed your brother Michael, and that your elder brother, Raphael, blamed you for it.'

Sammael nodded. 'Yes, it was a difficult time and I just couldn't stop blaming myself. I wouldn't listen to Gabriel when he said that something was very wrong with Raphael and that he may even have caused the accident that killed our youngest brother, Michael. We kept arguing, so I decided to leave Hobbes End and try and find some peace in wandering the Earth. Looking back on it now, all I was doing was running away. I had distanced myself so much from Hobbes End that I didn't know what was going on. If I had, I would have been here sooner. Please forgive me.'

Jonathan felt a strange twinge in his chest as he watched Sammael's face. She was doing a good job of maintaining her composure, but he knew that underneath the surface bubbled a whole lake of grief. The village told him so. He got up and walked across to his aunt and Sammael rose too, her eyes radiating loneliness. Knowing that it was the right thing to do, Jonathan wrapped his arms around Sammael and hugged her. He felt the intricate embroidery of the angel's dress press into his cheek, and realised that, just like Gabriel, Sammael had her own distinctive scent. Where Gabriel had smelled of apples and beeswax, Sammael carried with her the aroma of autumn bonfires, of fallen leaves, of a forest in winter.

'I forgive you,' said Jonathan. 'Just like my grandfather did.'

Sammael let out a huge, shuddering sigh, as if she were shrugging off a heavy load. She returned Jonathan's hug, gently cradling his head in one of her hands. 'Bless you,' she said softly. 'I have come home at last.'

Jonathan stepped back from Sammael. 'You've come home?'

She nodded. 'Yes, I've been here a few days already. I needed some time to . . . remember myself, and you needed time to recover from your wounds. Hobbes End has told me some of what occurred in my absence, but I need to know everything if I'm to be able to help. Tell me, Jonathan. Tell me your story.'

'What, now?'

'Yes,' said Sammael. 'Now is as good a time as any.'

They sat down, and Jonathan tried to tell his aunt what had happened to him in a way that made some sort of sense. In sharing his story he felt the burden of events begin to lift, and that felt good. He talked about the Corvidae's raid on his home and his father's capture by the archdemon Belial; about his mother's disappearance after leaving him in the protection of his grandfather, Gabriel, and the support he'd received ever since from everyone in the village. He described how the Corvidae had managed to cause havoc within Hobbes End, and how his grandfather had built a key to open a back door to Heaven in order to try and keep him safe.

'The wily old fox!' said Sammael with a smile. 'He actually built a secret door into Heaven when it was supposed to be impossible. He kept *that* close to his chest – I didn't know a thing about it.'

Jonathan nodded. 'My grandfather was full of secrets. The biggest is here on my wrist. A plain little watch; it gave me all of Gabriel's knowledge at the moment of his death, and using that I sent Belial back to Hell for Lucifer to deal with. It can also open that back door to Heaven I mentioned, if only I could figure out how to use it.'

Sammael puffed out her cheeks. 'Well, that is quite a tale,' she said. 'I wish I had seen your battle with Belial – it must have been magnificent.'

'It was,' said Ignatius. 'Although I doubt it's something anyone would wish to repeat.'

'And what about you, Cay?' asked Sammael.

Uncharacteristically shy at first, Cay told Sammael about coming to Hobbes End when she was a baby with her werewolf father and profoundly deaf mother. She told of her joy when she discovered a new friend in Jonathan, and shuddered when she described the attack by Raven, one of the Corvidae, who would have drowned her had it not been for her father and two gargoyles from the vicarage gates, Montgomery and Stubbs.

'Those two are worth their weight in granite,' said Sammael appreciatively.

'I sat with Gabriel when we were Belial's prisoners,' said Cay. 'He'd been blinded, but he never gave up. All I could do was try to be as brave as he was. He helped Jonathan save us all.'

Sammael gave Cay's hand a reassuring squeeze. 'You did far more than I, dear girl,' she said to Cay. 'You were by my brother's side in his darkest hour, and you did not fail him as I did. Bless you.' She turned to Ignatius and Grimm. 'And you, gentlemen, have you managed to have any adventures of your own?'

Ignatius nodded, and told her of how they had tried to keep Jonathan safe, and of the epic battle of Hobbes End where Rook and Raven of the Corvidae had finally been killed.

'We fought for our lives in the final battle against Belial,' said Ignatius. 'Me, Grimm and Cay's father in his wolf form. If it hadn't been for Gabriel's cunning and his sacrifice, we would be dead and Jonathan would be a slave. What's the point in getting old . . .'

'If you don't get crafty,' finished Sammael. 'Gabriel used to say that all the time, but I never understood how true it was.'

Ignatius smiled. 'I had been mourning the loss of my wife and little boy for such a long time. With Jonathan's arrival and everything that followed, Gabriel showed me what it was like to have a purpose again. I will always honour him for that.'

'I don't really have much to add, except to say that I'm obsessed with loose-leaf tea and I hit stuff with a cricket bat that I named after my first girlfriend,' Grimm joked.

Everyone burst into laughter, and the mood in the vicarage kitchen lifted. Despite everything that had happened, Jonathan suddenly felt that little bit lighter.

'So where've you been hiding yourself since you got here then, Mary Poppins?' said Elgar, peeping over the edge of his basket and grinning at Sammael.

'I – little demon – have been at home, listening to the heart-beat of the village. I hoped that Hobbes End would accept me now that my brother is no more, but I didn't want to assume.'

'And what did the village say?' asked Cay.

'It was nervous at first, but I think we have reached an understanding. Hobbes End likes having an archangel living in it, and it doesn't seem to be too unhappy that I'm the only candidate.'

'So where *have* you been living?' asked Grimm.

Sammael gave him a mischievous smile. 'All in good time, my dear Halcyon. I was going to come and see you all today anyway as I wanted to attend Gabriel's memorial service, but then last night something happened.'

Everyone went quiet.

'You felt it, didn't you, Jonathan?'

'You mean my nightmare?'

Sammael nodded. 'Yes, and it was no mere nightmare. It was a *sending*. Someone was calling out to you very strongly, and I think it may have been your father.'

'Do you really think so? He was in my dream, but he was with a boy angel,' said Jonathan. 'Everything was on fire and then Dad asked me to come and find him. But a horribly scarred angel grabbed hold of my leg and shouted at me to stay away. I actually woke up with a burn on my leg where he had touched me. What do you think it all means?'

'I'm not sure,' said Sammael, her forehead furrowed in thought. 'Dreams are strange things, but there's more than just your need to find your father at work here. There's something very powerful behind it.'

Jonathan's heart pounded in his chest. 'Can you help me find my dad?'

'I think so,' said Sammael. 'I know of a way to open a portal between Hobbes End and the steps of Heaven. It will be difficult, but I will make the attempt first thing tomorrow once I have rested and prepared myself; it's the least I can do to make up for my absence.'

Relief flooded through Jonathan. 'That's the best news I've heard in ages!' he said.

'Why will it be difficult for you to open a portal, Sam?' asked Cay.

The angel heaved a sigh. 'It's a bit complicated, but the upshot is that I no longer have access to my wings.'

'What do you mean?' asked Jonathan.

Sammael looked at him and paused, her face suddenly looking old and tired. She took a deep breath and spoke haltingly, as though the words were painful to utter. 'I no longer have access to my wings because I . . . I cut them off,' she said.

A Cruel and Unusual Punishment

With sunken eyes, Jonathan's mother stared at a grotesque throne of black basalt that was carved into the shape of a screaming angel. It radiated agony, desperation and despair. Seated on the throne was a towering, humanoid skeleton crowned with the skull of a gigantic horse. The bones were shot through with streaks of an unhealthy green, and the skeleton's huge hands clenched the arms of its throne in a vice-like grip. Deep in the empty eye sockets, a pale light flickered like the flame of a guttering candle.

'Well, well, Savantha,' said a voice from the darkness to her left. 'And how are you today? Are you enjoying your stay as my guest?'

Letting out a groan of pain Savantha turned her head towards the voice, laying her cheek against the slab of rock to which she was pinned. The slab reclined slightly, but it didn't afford her much ease. Her feet rested on the floor with her arms outstretched to either side, a long, thin shard of white crystal piercing each palm and pinning her securely to the stone. Her legs were so tired that she wanted nothing more than to let them relax, but every time she did so agony lanced through her hands.

'Show yourself, Baal,' Savantha demanded, her lips dry, her voice strained.

'Gladly,' said the voice. A young, incredibly handsome boy moved to stand in front of her. He was clad in a simple robe; his fair hair was tied at the back of his neck, and from his shoulders grew a pair of feathered angel's wings. He was perfect in every way except when he let his mask slip – it was then that Savantha could see the seething malice behind the boy's eyes.

'Please let me go,' she begged. 'All I want is to reach Lucifer and ask for his help to save my husband and my son.'

'I know, dear lady, but I couldn't have Lucifer interfering in my plans. It's why I've been holding you here all this time. I find myself with a problem, you see. Haven't you wondered why I'm speaking to you from the body of a young angel and not from my own true, magnificent form that sits upon the throne in front of you?'

Savantha nodded slowly.

'It's rather embarrassing really,' said Baal. 'I wanted to conquer Heaven, but I thought I'd try something new, something rather clever. Why go to all the trouble of laying siege to somewhere that is virtually impregnable, when I could just walk in and take over by stealth? I couldn't use my own body, of course – no amount of masking spells or shapechanging could hide my true nature from Heaven's gates – but what if I decided to build a body that I could use to enter Heaven undetected?'

Savantha's eyes widened.

'Ah, I see the penny begins to drop,' hissed Baal. 'I may not be quite as skilled as Gabriel in building machines of war, but that didn't matter. I created the construct of a perfect boy angel, and with great care and significant discomfort, have moved my soul inside it. After that it was easy. I walked into Heaven through the front door and slowly but surely made it mine. I'm the arch-demon of despair, and poor Raphael was so easy to control.'

'What have you done, you monster?' Savantha gasped.

'I have been playing a very long game,' said Baal. 'I rule Heaven and nobody has even noticed. Next I will take control of Hell, and after that, Earth itself. There will be nowhere in all of creation where you will not find despair. I have a problem however. Loath though I am to admit it, Raphael developed some backbone before I could put him out of his misery. With his last breath he cursed me – locked my soul in this hateful shell. I've tried to break free for so many years but to no avail. While my soul festers in this construct, buzzing around like a wasp in a jar, my real body begins to decay. You can see it, can't you? The rot creeping through my bones as I sit there, useless, on my throne.'

'Why are you telling me this?' Savantha begged.

'Because I want you to know what I'm going to do next,' said Baal. 'I want you to *despair*. The only thing that can free me is the power contained in the wing ribbons of an archangel, and unfortunately, they've become a bit thin on the ground. Sammael is a possibility, but she's very good at hiding, and after her fall from Heaven I don't know how much power she has left. Ironically I'd almost begun to despair myself . . . and then I heard about Jonathan.'

Savantha couldn't help but give an anguished sob.

'Good. You can see where I'm going with this now, can't you? I am going to lure Jonathan into Heaven, and when he is there, all alone in a strange place, I will *rip his wings from his shoulders and eat them*. Then, once my soul is back in its rightful home, you will see what I'm *truly* capable of.'

'Jonathan will stay in Hobbes End where he's safe,' said Savantha. 'There's no reason for him to go to Heaven.'

'Yes, well, that's where your husband comes in,' chuckled Baal. 'I found Darriel on the steps of Heaven where the Corvidae had left him. He was in a bit of a state, so I . . . looked after him. And then I had an idea. What if I dangled an injured Darriel in front of Jonathan? What wonderful bait *that* would be. Jonathan doesn't know where you are, dear lady, but suppose he had a dream in which his injured father begged him for help . . . well, he's going to do all he can to find him. Despite his . . . reduced circumstances, your husband somehow managed to interfere with my invitation to Jonathan, but he wasn't strong enough to stop me. Your little boy will come to Heaven to find his father, it's inevitable. And when he does I'll be waiting . . . to feed.'

Tears ran down Savantha's face and her chest heaved.

'And the best bit,' Baal continued, 'is that Jonathan appears to have a way into Heaven that doesn't involve going through the front gates. That means I don't have to leave them open to lure him in. I wouldn't want Lucifer finding out what I'm up to by taking a sneaky peek inside, now would I? I'm not sure of the details, but my spies tell me that Gabriel built a secret door that could be opened by a clock. I'm sure Jonathan will figure out the mechanism now that he has such a good incentive.'

'My son is strong enough to beat you,' Savantha whispered, her throat so dry she could barely make a sound.

'He may be able to put up a good fight,' said Baal, gloating, 'but unlike Belial I'm going to make sure Jonathan doesn't stand a chance, regardless of what power he may hold. I'll be bringing some help, you see.'

'What do you mean?'

'While I was in Heaven I took the time to do some exploring, and I found something very interesting indeed. I thought Gabriel would have destroyed them, but it seems that he couldn't bring himself to unmake his most terrible creations – his hollow angels, his Cherubim.'

Savantha squeezed her eyes shut and moaned.

'Ah, so you recognise the name? All demons do. The Cherubim were constructs of incredible power. At Gabriel's bidding they slaughtered the hordes of Hell at the battle of Armageddon. Just three man-shaped engines of destruction, but they were an army in themselves. After all this time they are not what they used to be, but I have made some modifications so that they will do my bidding. Look, Savantha,' he gloated, 'see what I have made to help me destroy your son!'

Unable to stop herself, Savantha opened her eyes as three figures stepped out of the shadows and lined up in front of her, their movements fluid and perfectly synchronous. Finally understanding what Jonathan was up against, despair overwhelmed her. The Cherubim smiled as she opened her mouth and gave vent to a cry of anguish that echoed around Baal's throne room.

Perambulations

'You cut your wings off?' said a stunned Jonathan.

Sammael sighed heavily. 'Yes. I had no choice. But now isn't the time for an explanation. I'll share my tale with you all later tonight, then you'll understand.'

Not wanting to cause Sammael further distress, everyone nodded their agreement.

'I think it's time I introduced myself to the current inhabitants of Hobbes End,' said the angel. 'Would you be so kind as to show me round for a bit?'

'Is that OK?' Jonathan asked Ignatius.

'Of course it is. Grimm and I have to go on a dragon hunt. Brass has gone missing, and given that she's Gabriel's largest and most dangerous construct, I'd like to know where she is.'

'How can you lose a dragon?' asked Elgar.

'We haven't lost her,' said Grimm. 'I think she's probably gone to find somewhere she can nest, as a pile of rubble can't be very comfortable.'

'I think I can help you there,' said Sammael. 'Brass is fast asleep at the bottom of the village pond.'

'Why on earth is she down there?' said Ignatius. 'I didn't think the pond would be deep enough to hide her.'

'She's down there because, just like Monty and Stubbs, she's a construct and needs to recharge. Sunlight would do it eventually, but at the bottom of the pond you have . . .'

'A huge battery powered by Gabriel's wings,' said Jonathan.

'Exactly,' said Sammael. 'By the time she wakes up she'll be a force to be reckoned with. And as for the pond, well, let's just say that the village wanted to accommodate Brass so it made the water deep enough for her to sleep in without being seen.'

'Hobbes End made the pond . . . deeper?' said Ignatius.

'Apparently so,' grinned Sammael. 'The village really is capable of some quite extraordinary things.'

Ignatius chuckled to himself and spun his empty pipe on the table. 'It never ceases to surprise me.'

'Right then,' said the angel. 'Let's be off. I really want to see the gargoyles.'

'Didn't they say hello when you came in?' asked Cay.

'I didn't want them to see me so I masked my presence. If they'd got all excited you'd have come out to have a look and that would have spoiled the surprise. It's sad, but I seem to have become very adept at blending into the background.'

Jonathan caught an edge of bitterness in his aunt's voice. There was much he didn't know about her, but he was determined to find out.

*

Bidding good morning to Ignatius and Grimm, Jonathan left the vicarage by the front door and walked down the drive. Accompanying him were Sammael, Elgar and Cay.

As usual Montgomery and Stubbs were facing the village green, but hearing the crunch of footsteps behind them they turned round and suddenly froze, their eyes wide and jaws sagging.

'There was me thinking you'd be all excited over my return,' said Sammael.

Stubbs hopped down from his perch and came to sit at the angel's feet, closely followed by Montgomery. 'Mistress,' they said, their voices brimming with a mixture of awe and extraordinary affection. 'We have missed you.'

'Am I having a stroke, or are they actually being deferential?' asked Elgar.

'Shhh!' Jonathan hushed the cat.

'I have missed you both too, my brave soldiers,' said Sammael. 'My brother Gabriel, working with Frederick Crumb, made you well, and they would be justly proud of your bravery. Oh look, Mr Stubbs, you're missing an ear.'

'Yeah,' nodded Stubbs. 'But you should see the other guy.' He grinned shyly and shuffled his feet.

'Have we done our duty?' asked Montgomery, his face serious.

Sammael dropped to one knee, cupped Montgomery's chin and looked him in the eyes. 'Above and beyond, both of you. You are as brave and strong as' – she paused – 'as brave and strong as a dragon.'

Jonathan smiled as the gargoyles' faces lit up with complete and utter joy.

'You *are* staying, aren't you?' they asked.

'Yes,' said Sammael. 'I'm home at last. No more wandering for me. Now, pop yourselves back on your posts; we can share our stories later. Right now I'm going to get myself reacquainted with Hobbes End.'

The gargoyles nodded excitedly and sprang back into position on either side of the gate. 'Reporting for duty, sir!' said Stubbs, coming to attention.

'Reporting for duty, *ma'am*,' corrected Montgomery.

'Sir!'

'Ma'am!'

'Oh, here we go again,' sighed Elgar. 'Can we go and look at something more interesting than two lichen-encrusted halfwits shouting at each other?'

Shaking her head, Sammael led Jonathan, Cay and Elgar through the gates. Behind them, the gargoyles continued their increasingly heated discussion over the correct form of address for a female commanding officer.

Jonathan cast a glance over his shoulder and looked at the stump of Stubbs's missing ear, knocked off by a falling block of stone during their hunt for Gabriel's Clock. It didn't seem fair that the little gargoyle should remain damaged, but with Gabriel gone there was nobody who knew how to build – or repair – constructs. *Unless I have a try*, Jonathan said to himself.

And I think I know just where to look for some help . . .

'Where would you like to go first?' Cay asked Sammael.

The angel slowed her stride for a moment and looked thoughtful. 'To my brother's cottage,' she said. 'It's where I last saw him and I would like to visit it again. The village told me that the cottage had suffered a bit recently and was apparently in need of some restoration.'

'On an understatement scale of one to ten, I'd say that was a forty-six,' said Elgar.

'What do you mean?' asked Sammael.

'You'll see when we get there.'

They continued their walk along the road by the green, under the ivy-covered roof of the lych gate and into the churchyard. As they went, Jonathan heard something at the back of his mind. It took him a moment to realise that it was Hobbes End singing happily to itself. Now that Sammael had introduced herself, the village didn't have to hide its true feelings.

He turned to see the angel looking at him, her eyebrows raised. 'You can hear it, can't you?'

Jonathan nodded. Somehow it seemed perfectly fitting that Hobbes End would sing to the sister of its creator now she had come home. Its song radiated happiness, contentment and peace. 'The village is really pleased you're here,' he said.

'I'm just surprised you can hear it so clearly,' said Sammael. 'You are half-demon, after all.'

'Ahem!' coughed Elgar. 'I hope you're not being demonist? I hail from all points demonic myself.'

'No offence, cat,' said Sammael.

'None taken,' he sniffed.

They continued on their way, the morning sun high and bright as they rounded the corner of the church to see a flattened mound of rubble and thatch. With Brass now residing at the bottom of the village pond, the churchyard seemed oddly empty.

'Ah, I see,' said Sammael. She heaved a big sigh and looked at the destruction. 'How did this happen?' she asked.

'When we came back from where Gabriel had hidden the fake clock, we had to leave in a bit of a hurry,' said Jonathan. 'Brass came with us and she had trouble squeezing through the door in Grandfather's attic. We sort of broke the cottage in the process. Sorry.'

Sammael shook her head, but the corner of her mouth turned up in the beginnings of a smile. 'That would explain the damage,' she said. 'Still, I'm glad you managed to find Brass. Gabriel was very fond of her and I'm pleased that she's safe. It's easier to build another cottage than build another dragon.'

Jonathan nodded.

'Hmm, I wonder what *that* is?' said Sammael, bending down to pull something from beneath a bundle of tattered thatch.

'What have you found?' asked Cay.

Sammael showed them: a small, battered, leather-bound book, with the words *High Flight* written on the cover in faded gold lettering. 'It's Gabriel's favourite book of poetry,' she said, gently brushing dust from the binding with her fingertips.

Jonathan looked at Sammael and saw tears gathering at the corners of her extraordinary eyes.

'Sentimental old fool,' the angel whispered, but not so quietly that Jonathan couldn't hear her. He wondered whether Sammael was referring to Gabriel, or to herself. 'Right then,' she added, wiping her eyes with a handkerchief she had tucked into her sleeve, 'how about we go to the village shop and say hello to your parents, Cay.'

'Oh, brilliant!' she said. 'Come on, let's go. Mum and Dad would love to meet you.'

It didn't take long to reach Cay's house. Outside, under the shop canopy, Joanne Forrester was arranging fruit and vegetables on a trestle table. She turned to see Cay and her friends approaching and smiled.

Sammael walked up to Joanne and surprised her by signing fluently. Cay couldn't see what Sammael said, but she watched as her mother's eyes went wide and filled with tears – not of sadness, but of deep joy and even deeper pride.

'What's going on?' growled a voice from inside the shop. Ducking his head to avoid the low canopy, Kenneth Forrester emerged from within, his beard bristling and a frown on his face as he saw his wife's apparent distress.

'It's all right,' Joanne signed to her husband. 'This is Sammael, Gabriel's sister. She came to thank us for what Cay did to help Gabriel before he died. The Morningstar has come home, beloved. There's nothing to be angry about.'

'Ah,' said Kenneth. 'I see. Then . . . welcome home, angel.'

Sammael inclined her head. 'Thank you, warrior,' she said.

'What's happening?' Jonathan asked Cay, unable to follow the signing between Sammael and Joanne.

'Sammael just thanked Mum and Dad for fighting for Hobbes End,' Cay whispered.

'Oh,' said Jonathan. 'That's good of her.'

'Yes,' said Cay, staring at the angel as she talked to her father. 'Yes, it is.'

Sammael finished her conversation and turned away. 'Well, I have a few things I need to finish up before the memorial service, but there is one more person I would like to see.'

'Who?' asked Cay.

'One of the few people who lived in Hobbes End at the same time as I last did. He's a private man but I'm quite fond of him. Now, I wonder . . . Ah! There he is, playing chess with that man with no socks on.'

'But that's Mr Peters and Professor Morgenstern,' said Cay. 'The professor hasn't been here as long as I have, so that means—'

'It means I've found the right person to speak to,' said Sammael happily.

Jonathan, Cay and Elgar trailed after the angel as she walked across the green towards the two men. They were seated on picnic chairs beneath a huge beech tree, and between them on a low table sat a chessboard. There were few pieces left in play and both men were deep in concentration. Mr Peters was dressed in his usual black clothes with little bare skin on show, and

Professor Horatio Morgenstern had once again forgotten to put his socks on.

'Hello, Vladimir,' said Sammael softly.

Mr Peters jumped up in surprise, knocking over the chessboard in the process. 'Is it really you?' he asked, peering at her from beneath the wide brim of his omnipresent hat.

Sammael nodded, and Mr Peters surprised everyone by bowing deeply. 'You return at a sad time, Morningstar,' he said.

'I know, old friend,' said the angel. 'My apologies for disturbing your game.'

'Ach! I was losing anyway. The professor is a worthy opponent.'

Horatio Morgenstern blinked and smiled, unsure of what was going on.

'I hope you don't mind, Professor, but I would like to borrow Vladimir if I may? It has been a long time since we had a chance to talk.'

'No, no, that's fine,' said the professor, gathering up the spilt chess pieces. 'I need to get back to work on my time machine anyway. I've given it a trial run but I lost the test guinea pig. A few tweaks are needed. Should be ready by Christmas.'

Sammael stared wide-eyed at the departing professor. 'A time machine?'

'Don't ask,' said Elgar, shaking his head. 'Ignatius is still trying to get him to hand over the hand grenades he made in case of an invasion.'

'I see,' said Sammael. 'Well, I'll catch up with you all later at the service. For now, I would like to speak with Vladimir.'

'OK,' said Jonathan. 'We'll see you then.'

Sammael gave him a gentle smile before turning and leaving with Mr Peters.

'Did she call him Vladimir?' asked Cay. 'See, I told you he was a vamp—'

Jonathan put a finger to Cay's lips. 'What did we say about that theory?'

Cay pouted. 'I still say he's undead,' she muttered under her breath.

'Well, what do we do for the rest of the day?' said Elgar.

Jonathan stared at his feet for a moment, but then gave his friends a huge grin. 'I want to try something if Stubbs will let me,' he said.

'Like what?' asked Cay.

'I'm going to see if I can fix his ear back on!'

The Library

'How are you going to fix an ear back on?' asked Elgar. 'I'm not sure,' said Jonathan as they strode back towards the vicarage. 'But I think I know where to find out. Remember last week when we were looking through those journals in Ignatius's study, to see if we could figure out how the Corvidae were getting into the village?'

'Yeah,' said Elgar.

'Well, in Frederick Crumb's journal there was a load of stuff about how he made the gargoyles, and there were notes from Gabriel too. Perhaps reading it will jog something in all that knowledge I've inherited from Gabriel and show me how to fix Stubbs.'

'It's worth a try,' said Cay. 'Assuming you can get Stubbs to agree.'

'Oh, he'll jump at the chance,' said Jonathan.

'Touch it and I will thump you soundly!' said Stubbs, hanging onto his broken ear for dear life while Montgomery tried to wrestle it from him.

'It's for your own good,' said Monty. 'Let Jonathan see if he can fix it.'

'Do I look like trial-run material?' protested Stubbs. 'I was built by an archangel and an experienced scientist.'

'An experienced scientist who blew himself and part of the vicarage up,' Cay reminded him.

'Well, yes, there was that,' said Stubbs. 'But I'm not convinced. Reattaching my ear requires a lot more finesse than giving an archdemon a good kicking.'

'Trust me, Stubbsey,' said Jonathan. 'I just need to read through these notes, and if I understand them then I'll fix you. I won't risk doing anything unless I'm sure, OK?'

Stubbs frowned. 'Well . . . if you think it's a good idea,' he said, reluctantly handing his broken ear to Jonathan. 'But if you reattach it at a *jaunty angle* or anything that isn't perfectly straight, we will have *words*!'

'I understand,' said Jonathan, doing his best to soothe the frightened gargoyle. 'Just give me a minute to get ready.'

Stubbs sat down, crossed his arms and gazed disconsolately over the still water of the village pond. 'Fine,' he huffed. 'You read the instruction manual. I'll just sit here and wait to be made a laughing stock.'

Jonathan shook his head and smiled. Sitting cross-legged on the grass, he opened the journal of Frederick Crumb that he had borrowed from the bookcase in Ignatius's study. He had chosen this spot to attempt the repair because it was as close as he could get to the heart of Hobbes End – the sheet of black glass at the bottom of the pond that held the power of Gabriel's wings. Despite his outward confidence and the reassuring presence of his friends, Jonathan knew that he needed all the help he could get. He hoped that being so close to a part of his grandfather might assist him.

Turning to the pages that detailed the construction of Monty and Stubbs, he tried his best to make sense of what he found there. On the surface, the diagrams and formulae, lists and instructions were nigh-on incomprehensible, but Jonathan was not just anyone – his blood sang with the power that came from being a mix of angel and demon, and somewhere in his head lay a vast storehouse of information bequeathed to him by Gabriel.

As Jonathan read the faded lettering on the pages, the world about him began to fall away. His friends' voices faded to a gentle murmur, and he found himself somewhere new. He could still feel the grass beneath his legs and the breeze on his face, but it was as if he straddled two worlds, one physical, and one purely inside his head.

In front of him lay a vast, ornate library, lit from above by starlight shining through a glass ceiling. Beautiful oak bookcases stretched off in all directions with galleries to either side. There were sliding ladders to help reach the higher shelves, and in the centre was a circular desk with a green-glass reading lamp.

Jonathan knew that the library was his way of interpreting all the information that Gabriel's Clock had given him, but he was also aware of a big problem; where to look? Incredible though the library was, it had no apparent filing system, and that frustrated Jonathan. He knew that understanding comes with experience, but that took time, and once again time was what he didn't have if he was going to save his father, find his mother and repair a reticent gargoyle.

'Right,' he said to himself. 'Where are you?'

With half his waking mind scanning Frederick's journal, and the other half walking through an imaginary library, Jonathan asked himself a question – how do you fix the broken ear of a little granite construct?

He walked along one avenue of bookcases, and then back down another, each time leaving and returning to the space occupied by the circular reading desk, but nothing seemed to happen. All the books were beautifully bound but their spines were blank. Jonathan knew that if he just pulled them out at random he would probably die of old age before he found what he was looking for – providing he could understand what was in the books anyway.

He pulled out a solitary chair and sat at the reading desk, aware that his friends were also sitting by the pond and waiting for him to pull a rabbit out of a hat. He had just begun to think he'd made a fool of himself when he had an idea. If the library was his mind's way of making sense of all the knowledge given to him by Gabriel, then surely he could ask it to help him find what he needed, or at least to give him a clue as to where it was hidden.

Jonathan focused on his desire to repair Stubbs. At the same time he imagined himself holding the severed ear, bringing it closer to Stubbs's head while willing the roughly-broken edges to flow into each other, to fuse solid until the ear was as good as new. He imagined the happiness on Stubbs's face, the dance of joy the gargoyles would likely do when they felt that things had gone well, and the sense of satisfaction that he would feel at having achieved such a small but wonderful thing. This is my intention, Jonathan thought to himself.

He looked up from the desk, his vision pulled towards a distant shelf on an upper gallery. There, tucked away in a corner, the spine of a single, slim volume was glowing faintly, sparkling in the starlight. He leaped up and ran to the nearest spiral staircase, his feet thundering on the steps as he pelted upward. Once he'd reached the gallery, he grabbed the nearest sliding ladder and pulled it level with the glowing book. Clambering up the rungs, he reached out and slid his prize from the shelf. Clutching it tightly to his chest, Jonathan sprinted back to the reading desk.

He sat down and with mounting excitement looked at the book he had chosen. The spine had ceased to glow, and in its place a book title had appeared. It read:

A treatise on sub-atomic crystalline mechanics
Or, Constructs for dummies

Jonathan chuckled. Not only did it appear that he had the right book, but it even gave itself a title that he could understand. He opened it to the first page and ran the tip of his finger along the printed words of the opening line. As he watched, the ink ran off the paper, up his finger and across the back of his hand. Images flashed across his vision as the contents of the book flowed into his mind and made themselves understood.

Before Stubbs could react, Jonathan reached out and placed the severed part of the gargoyle's ear against the jagged stump on his head. Time froze as Jonathan focused his will on the damaged stone, his senses zooming in on the task until he felt himself surrounded by a lattice of particles and energy fields. But there was more than just structure, there was personality written into every atom, everywhere around him was Stubbs.

Jonathan understood the nature of the challenge he faced. Anyone could just glue an ear on a stone statue, but it wouldn't be the same, living stone that made the gargoyles what they were. It would be like gluing a joke ear onto a human. It might look the same, but it would be lifeless, unconnected to the whole. Desperate to avoid such an outcome, Jonathan called to the formulae that his grandfather had written down when he had helped Frederick Crumb build Monty and Stubbs.

The insanely complex mathematics became like clay in his hands and he used it to smooth, to join and to mend. The stone of the severed ear grew hot, and in a million places sparks of energy leaped between it and its proper place on Stubbs's head. Finally, the two surfaces locked together, blazed white, and Jonathan knew that he had succeeded. With a huge sigh he fell back onto the grass, spots of light dancing before his eyes.

There was silence. Jonathan propped himself up on his elbows to see Elgar, Cay and Montgomery looking at him open-mouthed. At Jonathan's feet, an incredulous Stubbs was hesitantly tapping his reattached ear as if he couldn't quite believe it was fixed.

The little gargoyle stared at Jonathan with an expression of utter hero-worship. He wrung his hands and burbled, so overcome that he was unable to say anything that made sense. Montgomery came to his aid.

'What Mr Stubbs is trying to say,' said Montgomery, putting a calming arm round his friend's shoulders, 'is that he is profusely overcome with gratitude for the repairs you administered to his damaged appendage, and begs forgiveness for inferring that your efforts would only befit an amateur.' He turned to Stubbs. 'Did I cover everything?'

Stubbs nodded vigorously, his bottom lip quivering as he tried not to blub.

'Thanks, Stubbsey, it was my pleasure,' said Jonathan.

'You did it!' cried Cay. 'You actually *did* it!'

'I am officially impressed,' said Elgar. 'You've managed to render Stubbs speechless. No mean feat.'

Jonathan nodded, genuinely happy at what he'd done.

'How did you figure out what to do?' asked Cay.

'I was talking to Ignatius about it last night,' said Jonathan. 'I was telling him that when I think about all Gabriel's knowledge, it's like I'm walking in a huge library, but I don't know where the information I'm looking for is kept.'

'So how did you find what you needed?' asked Cay.

'I just . . . I just thought really hard about what I wanted to achieve, and the library pointed the way. I just somehow knew what I had to do after that.'

'That's genius!' beamed Cay. 'Do you think you could ask the library how Gabriel's Clock can open that back door into Heaven?'

Jonathan's mouth sagged open as the importance of what she had just said sunk in. Much to Cay's surprise he flung his arms round her and kissed her on the cheek. 'Oh, that's brilliant!' he gasped. 'Of course I can. If I can mend Stubbs's ear I must be able to figure out how this little watch works. If Sammael can't open the main gates to Heaven tomorrow, then I'm not stuck. I can get in the back way, just like Gabriel wanted. I can find Dad and then Mum!'

Cay hugged him back. 'Yeah,' she said softly. 'You can finally go and find your parents.'

'You know,' said Elgar, grinning so widely it looked as though the top of his head might fall off, 'I love it when a plan comes together.'

In Memoriam

L ater that evening, the air was warm and filled with scent from the ancient wisteria which clung to the stone of St Michael's. All of Hobbes End was gathered in a churchyard filled with lanterns, their warm light holding back the dusk. It had been a week since the death of the archangel whose fall from grace had created their sanctuary, and now it was time for the villagers to properly say goodbye.

In a far corner, near to the grave of Ignatius's wife and son, a slab of white marble had been laid flush with the closely-mown grass. It was plain, but polished to such a degree that it looked like a pool of water. Inscribed upon it in elegant script were the words:

Gabriel Artificer
Brother, Father, Archangel
Genius
'For I have slipped the surly bonds of earth
And danced the skies on laughter-silvered wings'

Jonathan stood next to Sammael, rolling the words over in his mind. He had barely met his grandfather before he lost him, and that hurt more than he could explain. The pain was softened by two things: a simple watch that he now wore on his left wrist; and buried deep inside his head, the accumulated knowledge of the greatest engineer the universe had ever seen.

'What do you think?' asked Sammael.

'I like it,' said Jonathan. 'I think Gabriel would too. Did it take you long to make?'

'A couple of days; I'm more used to working with glass than I am with stone, but I think he would approve. We often worked on projects together. Only once did we regret what we had created.'

'You mean the Cherubim?' asked Jonathan.

Sammael nodded, her face sad. 'Did Gabriel tell you about them?'

'Yeah,' said Jonathan. 'He said he made them to help Heaven fight against Lucifer's army at the battle of Armageddon. He called them his hollow angels.'

'That's a very apt description,' said Sammael. 'They looked almost human but they had no souls. They were engines of destruction under our control and without them we would have been crushed. I truly wish they hadn't been so necessary. I think seeing something so magnificent cause so much death almost broke Gabriel's heart. Let us hope we never see their like again.'

Jonathan reached out and took his aunt's hand.

'Everyone's here,' Cay said softly as she appeared next to them.

He turned round and saw a crowd of people standing respectfully behind him; each one was holding a lantern and waiting to say farewell to the old archangel who had given them a place to be safe. Monty and Stubbs were there too, perched on the churchyard wall with their heads bowed.

Jonathan, Sammael and Cay stepped back to join the crescent of villagers as Ignatius began the service. He spoke of growing up in the vicarage, and how incredible it had been to find out that an archangel lived next door. Other villagers followed, all sharing their experiences of Gabriel, of his kindness, his love and his sacrifice.

Sammael walked forward to stand next to Gabriel's memorial. Once there she turned to face the assembled crowd. 'I am Sammael Morningstar,' she said. 'On behalf of my brother, I thank you for the honour you have shown him this night. Were he watching he would probably have grumbled about it being overly sentimental, but in his heart he would have been touched beyond measure.'

A ripple of laughter spread through the villagers.

'Some of you have already met me, and I hope to get a chance to speak to all of you soon. I cannot replace my brother, but I will try my best to continue his legacy. My days of wandering are over, and I would like to make Hobbes End my home.'

A gentle round of applause met her declaration, and Jonathan smiled as he saw his great-aunt actually blush.

'Are you finally going to tell us where you'll be living?' asked Grimm, a cheeky grin on his face.

'I thought you might ask that, my dear Halcyon,' said Sammael looking up at the night sky. 'It's a full moon tonight, and a perfect time to show you my home. If everyone would kindly follow me, I have something you may like to see.'

An excited Sammael led the way out of the churchyard. Behind her – buzzing with curiosity – came the villagers.

'My paws are wet,' Elgar huffed. 'My mother warned me about damp grass, said it'd give me piles.'

'Oh, for goodness' sake!' growled Grimm, the light from his lantern illuminating their path across the village green as they strode along.

'Is he always like this?' Sammael asked Ignatius, her arm linked through his as they walked.

'Elgar or Grimm?' said Ignatius.

'The cat,' Sammael chuckled.

'Oh, this is him in a good mood,' said Ignatius, chewing on the stem of his pipe. 'If he's in a real temper, I suggest you check your shoes before putting them on – you never know what little present he may have left in them.'

'That wasn't my fault,' said Elgar, glaring at Ignatius. 'It was you who shut me in the hall cupboard; where was I supposed to go?'

'Point taken,' said Ignatius, trying to suppress a grin.

The edge of the forest drew near, and after climbing a small rise the inhabitants of Hobbes End reached a wide area of cleared scrub. In the middle was a pile of rotting logs, the remnants of trees that had been cut down years earlier.

'Here we are,' said Sammael. 'What do you think?' she asked Elgar, her eyes glittering in the moonlight.

'Nice logs,' said the cat.

'They weren't your house or anything, were they?' asked Grimm. 'I've been using bits of them for years to lay fires back at the vicarage.'

'No,' Sammael reassured him. 'They weren't my house. *This* is my house.'

Removing the glove from her left hand, she extended her forefinger and drew a vertical line in the night air, from high above her head down to the earth at her feet. There was a sudden ripping noise, like a cross between the zip on a tent being rapidly undone and fingernails being raked down a blackboard. Elgar shuddered as his fur stood on end, and Jonathan and Cay winced as the sound shredded across their nerves like a cheese grater.

'What the—?' Ignatius gasped, as what up until now had been reality dropped to the ground like a torn theatre curtain. Behind it was something quite extraordinary.

Jonathan stared open-mouthed while Elgar jumped onto Grimm's shoulders to get a better look. Where for years there had been nothing but scrub and rotting wood, a huge black tower now reared against the night sky. Skeletal shapes passed in front of the moon with a rhythmic creak and swish, and empty stone eye sockets gaped blindly in the dark. It was a windmill.

Grimm shone the beam of his lantern upward. 'How . . . who . . . when?' he spluttered, before giving up and just gawping.

'But this burned down before I was born, didn't it?' Ignatius asked Sammael.

'That's what everyone was supposed to think,' she replied. Striding forward, she placed her hand on the wooden door in front of her. On every windowsill, a small, glass-shrouded candle burst into life, pushing back the darkness to welcome Sammael home.

Jonathan watched transfixed as the huge, slatted, wooden sails turned almost silently in front of him, each one glowing a ghostly silver as it passed in front of the moon. From his vantage point on Grimm's shoulders, Elgar turned his head this way and that, stunned at the change. One minute he'd been paw-deep in old bracken, the next he was in the middle of an unkempt flower garden, surrounded by a privet hedge in desperate need of a trim.

'Welcome to my home,' said Sammael, unable to keep the joy from her voice as she saw the astonishment on her new friend's faces. 'Mind your head as you come in!'

A History Lesson

The inhabitants of Hobbes End were pleasantly stunned to have a windmill suddenly appear in their village. They crowded into the overgrown garden that surrounded the building and marvelled at the silhouette of Sammael's home against the bright moon. Monty and Stubbs couldn't resist grabbing onto the ends of the sails and letting themselves be hoisted aloft on their own, private fairground ride. Nobody seemed to notice that the sails were turning despite the absence of a breeze.

Jonathan observed that the only person who didn't seem surprised at Sammael's revelation was Mr Peters. The old man was smiling, and looking at the windmill in a way that suggested he was remembering what it had looked like before Sammael had hidden it. How old are you really? Jonathan thought.

Sensing he was being watched, Mr Peters turned and gave Jonathan a conspiratorial wink.

'Who would like tea?' boomed Grimm, poking his head out of the windmill's door. Everyone's hand went up. 'I was afraid of that,' he sighed, before turning to confer with Sammael. Ten minutes later, the garden was covered with lanterns and blankets and everyone was chatting, drinking and eating an extraordinary amount of custard creams.

'Have you been stashing them away for just such an occasion, Sam?' asked Elgar.

'I'd be fibbing if I said no,' replied Sammael. 'I hoped that I would fit in here, but this is a welcome that exceeds my expectations. A large tin of Earl Grey and a few packets of biscuits are a small price to pay.'

The angel moved about her garden, greeting everyone and making them all welcome. Jonathan sat on a wooden bench next to Cay and studied Sammael as she played host. 'Does she seem a bit happier than she was this morning?' he asked.

Cay glanced up from her tea and watched the angel for a moment. 'Yes, she is. I think she was worried about being accepted, but now she knows that everything is going to be OK.'

Jonathan nodded, but as for everything being OK, tomorrow morning couldn't come fast enough. His need to find his parents was becoming all-consuming and he wouldn't accept any more delay.

The night drew on, and after the villagers had packed up and made their way to their respective cottages, Sammael, Ignatius, Grimm, Jonathan, Cay and Elgar sat around a large wooden table inside the windmill. Monty and Stubbs had returned to guarding the vicarage, and Cay's parents, knowing that their daughter would be most upset if she were made to go home, were perfectly happy to let her stay in Jonathan's company for as long as she wanted.

The circular room in which they sat was dominated by a slowly rotating wooden beam that stretched from floor to ceiling. Jonathan could see the where the huge granite millstones would have sat on a floor now covered with polished slate tiles. Sammael reached out and brushed the turning beam with her fingers. 'Rest now,' she whispered. With a gentle sigh, the sails lost their momentum, and the mechanism came to a halt.

'Atchoo!' sneezed Elgar, dust tickling the inside of his nose.

'Yes, the old place does need a thorough clean, doesn't it?' said Sammael. 'I've been away for such a long time.' The angel went silent, the only noise in the room coming from the cast-iron stove as the burning wood inside it popped and crackled.

'But you're home now,' said Ignatius, 'and we need you to be the Morningstar again. Tell us *your* story, Sammael; help us understand what happened to your family.'

The angel sighed heavily. 'Yes,' she said. 'It's time I tried to make peace with myself.' She sat back in her chair, staring into the orange flames flickering inside the stove. 'It all began with Lucifer,' she started. 'Formed by creation's desire to see life, light and order, he stood alone against an infinite, freezing void filled with darkness and monsters. Then he spoke the words that had been given to him and chaos was driven back.'

'*Let there be light,*' said Ignatius with a smile.

Sammael nodded. 'Lucifer means *bringer of light*, and he shone so very brightly. After seeing our universe born he slept for aeons, and when he awoke he was given the task of building Heaven. He didn't have to do it alone though, for he found that nine hundred and ninety-nine other archangels had also been created.

They became known as the *Araelim*, and together they built a city of stone and glass, hanging in space like a teardrop from the eye of God. It was magnificent.

'Once they had finished their labours the archangels began to have families, but none of their children had the same wings or extraordinary powers. Only the Araelim had ribbons of light they could summon from their shoulders; their children, the *Seraphim*, had wings with feathers.'

'But you had wing ribbons, didn't you?' asked Jonathan. 'And so did Grandfather. Were both of you Araelim too?'

'No,' said Sammael. 'Our family seems to be a bit of an anomaly, but I'll get to that in a minute. Heaven prospered for a time, and we did our best to keep an insignificant little planet called Earth safe from demon predation. Its inhabitants were special, you see. To my knowledge they are the only sentient life in all of creation, outside of Heaven and Hell.'

'So aliens don't exist then?' asked Elgar.

'Much as I would like them to, no, they don't,' chuckled Sammael. 'Still, for a long time everything was perfect.' She sighed. 'But then things began to unravel.'

'What went wrong?' asked Cay.

'I'm not sure,' replied the angel. 'I was only a baby at the time, but it seems that Lucifer was not content with Heaven maintaining a status quo. He wanted to expand, to explore, to create life on other worlds.'

'He wanted to play God,' said Grimm.

Sammael nodded. 'Lucifer was very persuasive. He turned half the population of Heaven against the other and a brutal civil war began. Through the bravery of Uriel – the most senior of the Araelim after Lucifer – we prevailed, but the cost was terrible. Uriel lived just long enough to see Lucifer chained and exiled to Hell before he finally died from his injuries. And with him gone the Araelim were no more – only Seraphim remained to pick up the pieces. The war created many orphans, all crying out for their lost parents, and among the ranks of those poor children were new-born quadruplets.'

'Four babies?' said Jonathan.

'Yes,' she said. 'There was me, Sammael Morningstar, and my brothers Gabriel Artificer, Raphael Executor, and Michael Hellbane. Strangest of all, these babies born of Araelim parents were able to manifest wing ribbons: something that had never happened before. It's almost as if creation knew we would be needed and so arranged for us to be there.

'As my brothers and I grew we helped the remaining Seraphim to rebuild Heaven. We hoped that we would see nothing but peace from then on, but it was not to be. In time Lucifer rose up against us, the legions of Hell at his back, his pride so great he couldn't see the damage he was doing to creation.

'Although heavily outnumbered, we had a secret weapon. Gabriel built three constructs to help us, each powered by a wing ribbon cut from his own back. He forged them in the heart of the sun from an alloy of metal and glass while I shielded him from the fire. They were the Cherubim – the hollow angels, and they were destruction incarnate.'

Jonathan shivered. In his mind he could feel the awful heat on Gabriel's face, smell the burning skin of his hands, feel the gnawing desperation in his grandfather's heart as he built something he knew he would come to regret. Jonathan saw Sammael hanging in space, wreathed in fire, her eyes ablaze and the look on her face exultant as Gabriel finished his deadly work, trusting his sister to shield him from the sun's fury. Jonathan remembered the way his grandfather had described Sammael: *she's special, you see. She's immune to the heat and radiation of a star; the rest of us are not.*

Sammael's voice softened almost to a whisper. 'When we faced the enemy that awful day they had no idea what was coming. Lucifer and the archdemons – Belial, Baal and Lilith – were so sure of themselves. Their army was vast, and Heaven was still recovering from the civil war that Lucifer had caused. We were so few, and they laughed at us as we lined up to fight. We opened ranks and Michael – the spear that I'd made for him gripped tightly in his hand – charged, the Cherubim at his side. At first the demons didn't understand what was happening; they just stood there, not realising that death was moments away. Then the Cherubim spread their lethal wings and the killing began. When I say that the edges of their wings were sharp, I don't really do them justice. They were so thin they could almost cut light.'

Elgar mewled quietly and put his paws over his eyes. 'My parents told me about this,' he said. 'I heard it was a legend; but it really happened, didn't it?'

Sammael nodded, and, putting down her tea she picked Elgar up and sat him on her lap, stroking his fur to comfort herself as much as the cat.

'I remember the screaming,' the angel continued, her voice quiet and sad. 'And those awful wet noises. The wrath of Heaven cut down the demon army like wheat before a scythe.' She pursed her lips and rubbed the fingertips of her right hand against her forehead. 'With Hell in disarray we charged after Michael, our only thought to destroy everything in our path. It wasn't until I was standing knee-deep in bodies that I realised what was happening – we'd become just like the demons. All about me was fighting and screaming and death. It was then that I heard someone shout out a word, and it was a shout filled with such command that everyone – angel, demon, even the Cherubim – turned to listen.'

'What was the word?' asked Jonathan.

'*STOP!*' said Sammael. 'It was Lucifer. He was standing nearby, his armour and sword drenched in blood. He had this expression of revulsion on his face and I realised that despite what he was trying to do, he was as sickened by the slaughter as I was. We both looked at each other and knew what we had to do. For if we didn't, there'd be nothing left for the victor but ash.'

'You fought each other to decide the battle, didn't you?' said Jonathan.

Sammael nodded. 'We fought and we fought. For how long I don't know. Hours? Days? But at the end I held my sword to Lucifer's throat and the war was over. There'd be no more fighting between Heaven and Hell, ever. And in that awful silence after the storm, I heard the sound of a broken soul.'

'Raphael?' said Cay.

'Yes,' said Sammael. 'I'm sure Gabriel told you what happened. I knew the voice that was crying out as though it were my own. I followed its pain across the battlefield until I found my brother. He was kneeling on churned and bloody ground, cradling the body of his beloved Bethesda. She was dead. They were going to be married, you know? He and Beth, the gentlest of the gentle. Raphael looked at me and in his eyes I could see despair blossom. All that was good in him ripped out to lie bleeding next to Beth. He shouted at me to finish the demons off, to let the Cherubim slaughter them all, every man, woman and child. I refused.'

'Dear God,' said Ignatius, holding a hand to his mouth in disbelief.

'And so we buried the dead and went home, never to be the same again. Raphael locked himself away, grief tearing him apart; and Gabriel, horrified at the carnage wrought by the Cherubim, locked them away and swore never to use them again. Only my brother Michael was still his old self. He had a mighty heart, that boy, and he helped me with all the work that needed to be done. And as reward for his loyalty' – her voice shook a little – 'I ended up killing him.'

'But Gabriel said it was an accident,' said Elgar. 'It wasn't your fault!'

'Dear Gabriel,' sighed the angel. 'He always did think the best of me. Did he tell you the truth of what happened?'

'He said that Michael thought you were in trouble,' said Jonathan. 'That he was rushing to come and save you, just as you created a new star.'

Sammael nodded. 'Yes. My last star. We had jobs, you see, my siblings and I. Creation wasn't quite finished; it needed tweaking and polishing, and that was our role, to ensure that creation was as perfect as it could be. Raphael instinctively knew where changes needed to be made, and it was usually Gabriel that solved those problems. However, now and again there would be a gap where for some reason a star should have formed, but didn't, and that's where I came in. Through the windows of my wings I could start the chain reaction that would give birth to a new sun – it's why I'm called Morningstar.'

'And what was Michael's job?' asked Cay.

Sammael smiled. 'His role was to look after us all, without fear or favour. He was our guardian, and nothing would stop him if he thought one of his siblings was in danger – it was his greatest weakness. He thought I was in trouble so he did something foolish. He tore a hole in the fabric of creation so he could appear at my side – just as I opened my arms and felt the star blossom around me. I could see the look of horror on his face as he was vaporised.'

Her voice broke for a moment. 'I never understood why he thought I was in danger,' she said. 'There was no reason for him to be there.' She shook her head sadly. 'I made my way back to Heaven and told Raphael what had happened. Michael's death added to the horror of the war against Lucifer, and I just felt numb.

'Raphael had the right to pass judgement on my crime, so pass judgement he did. In the past he would have shown mercy, but the loss of Beth and my refusal to continue the war had made him hate me. After sentencing me to exile my brother wrapped me in chains of star-forged glass, dragged me to the gates of Heaven and threw me into the abyss. The fall from grace is a long one, and as I hurtled earthward I began burning. I could have shielded myself, stopped the pain, but I chose not to – I couldn't let myself go unpunished. In my grief I surrendered my wings to the flames, voluntarily doing what even the heart of a star could not. And so I struck the earth, somewhere in Siberia, I think. I believe that scientists have credited the impact crater to a meteorite strike.' She grinned ruefully.

'And your wings,' said Jonathan. 'This morning you said that you cut them off.'

'Yes,' sighed the angel. 'By this point my wings were virtually useless, so great was the damage visited upon them. I walked alone for decades, hoping they would heal, but they didn't. My guilt over Michael's death made me question whether I deserved to have all that power back again anyway. I finally realised that while my wings were with me, they would never have a chance of repairing themselves. And then I heard Gabriel cry out as he too fell from Heaven. Lonely and desperate, I made my way to where he'd landed, only to find out he had built himself a home. Because he had exiled himself, unchained and of his own free will, his wings did not suffer the level of damage that mine had. And yet he still gave most of his power away to create this village, to build a place of refuge. I loved him for that.'

'But . . .' Jonathan interrupted.

'I know, I know. What happened to my wings?'

Jonathan nodded and everyone leaned forward, wondering what Sammael would reveal next.

'It was Gabriel who had the idea,' said Sammael. 'He had been able to cut off three of his wing ribbons to power the Cherubim, although the process was excruciatingly painful. He suggested that if my wings were to have a chance to heal, then they needed to be removed and stored where they could slowly absorb sunlight.'

'So what did you do?' asked Cay.

'I kneeled on this very floor and Gabriel cut my wing ribbons from me. The pain was . . . significant. And it wasn't just physical pain; it was as if I was losing a precious part of myself. You can still see the gouge-marks my fingers made on the flagstones before I passed out.'

Jonathan looked down at the floor, and sure enough there were two hand-shaped patches of damaged tiles. He wondered just how much pain was required to render an archangel unconscious. 'And what did you do with your wing ribbons?' he asked Sammael, his own shoulders aching with phantom discomfort.

'I'm very good at working with glass, and with Gabriel's help I built a vessel in which to house my precious wings,' she said, smiling at her nephew.

'And where is it?' he asked, returning her smile.

'It's hanging on the wall behind you,' she said, nodding to somewhere over Jonathan's right shoulder.

Everyone swivelled round to follow the angel's gaze. There, hanging from a length of stout cord, was a large mirror. The frame was expertly cut from ebony, and as they watched, the glass grew dark, their stunned reflections disappearing into a caged maelstrom of swirling blackness. A simulacrum of Sammael's face appeared briefly in the glass, winked, then faded away.

'My wings are a bit like Hobbes End,' chuckled Sammael. 'But they don't have the degree of sentience required to be truly alive. They're just a part of me trapped inside a glass prison, waiting for their parole.'

'And have they healed over the centuries?' asked Grimm, his eyes goggling at the mirror.

'I don't know,' said Sammael. 'That mirror has hung on the wall for a very long time, looking out the window and drinking in the sunlight of a thousand summer days. My wings seem more alive than when I hung the mirror there, but . . . as to whether they are healed, there is no way of telling until I break the glass. And if they are not healed, then without Gabriel's help I have no immediate way of trying again. My wings might just fade and die before we could build somewhere else to house them.'

'But you don't know that,' said Jonathan. 'They might be perfectly restored and you could be an archangel again.'

'I may have cut off my wings,' said Sammael, 'but I never stopped being an archangel.'

Jonathan hung his head. 'I'm sorry,' he said. 'I didn't mean to be rude.'

His aunt reached over and squeezed his hand. 'No offence taken,' she said. 'Once you have mastered your grandfather's knowledge, then maybe we can risk opening the mirror, see whether I can once again touch the face of God.'

'That would be amazing,' said Jonathan. 'You've waited such a long time. I hope I can help one day.'

'You will,' said Sammael.

'Aren't you worried about someone stealing the mirror?' asked Elgar.

'It did cross my mind,' said Sammael. 'That's why I hid the windmill when I last left Hobbes End. Besides, anyone stealing the mirror will find that it's not as fragile as it looks. There's only one way to get to my wings and I'm keeping that very secret!'

'Fair enough,' said the cat.

Sammael got up and walked towards the kitchen. 'I think I'll put the kettle on. After all that talking I fancy another cup of—' She stopped in mid-stride, her face turned towards the windmill's front door.

Jonathan looked at her and his heart froze. His aunt's face had lost all colour and her expression was one of shock.

'What is it, Sam?' he asked, getting out of his chair and going to her.

The angel gulped. 'We have a visitor,' she said, her voice rasping through a dry mouth.

There was a sudden knocking on the door. Three firm and perfectly interspaced raps. 'Who is it?' everyone asked at once.

'The old adversary,' whispered Sammael.

Ignatius got up too, his face as pale as Sammael's. 'While listening to your tale I hadn't noticed how quiet Hobbes End had gone,' he said. 'Can it really be him?'

Sammael nodded. 'He's even better than me at going unnoticed unless he wants to be. Given that he's a fallen angel as opposed to an archdemon, I assume Hobbes End isn't sure what to make of him! Well, there's no point annoying him by leaving him outside. He clearly wants to come in.'

She walked over to the door and opened it.

'Hello, Lucifer,' she said.

Better the Devil You Know:
Part Two

Jonathan stood and watched as a man emerged from the darkness outside the windmill. He was tall and handsome, and was wearing an immaculately cut suit with a white shirt and black silk tie. His wavy hair was silver-grey, and above a neatly trimmed salt-and-pepper beard, dark eyes regarded the room from either side of an aquiline nose.

'Good evening,' he said, nodding politely at the group of faces that stared at him in disbelief. 'Is that Earl Grey brewing in the pot? May I?'

Grimm hesitantly poured a cup for Lucifer as Sammael addressed their guest. 'To what do we owe this unexpected pleasure?' she asked him.

'If you let me sit down I'll tell you,' Lucifer replied, the merest hint of a smile tugging at the corner of his mouth.

Jonathan watched as Ignatius, his discomfort obvious, pulled out a chair.

Lucifer sat down and took a sip of his tea. 'Now then,' he said, 'I'm sure you're all wondering why I'm here.'

'The thought is uppermost in all our minds,' said Sammael, retaking her seat at the table, closely followed by Jonathan.

'I came to pay my respects,' said Lucifer. 'I admired Gabriel greatly. I wished to attend his memorial service as a mark of respect for one whose like we may never see again.' He flicked his gaze briefly toward Jonathan.

Jonathan felt himself pinned to his chair by Lucifer's sudden attention – it only lasted a second, but it felt like an eternity. He didn't need his rapidly growing link with Hobbes End to sense how powerful their visitor was. Vast pride was mixed with an extraordinary intelligence, and it was like sitting next to a bomb that could go off at any moment. Lucifer looked away and Jonathan sagged in his chair with relief.

'I did not wish to intrude or cause distress to the inhabitants of this village so I remained at a distance,' Lucifer continued. 'I heard what you said during the service, Sammael, and I agree. Gabriel *would* have called you sentimental, but deep down he would have been pleased.'

'Thank you,' she said, genuinely touched.

'Not at all. Gabriel was almost as clever as me, and that level of skill requires acknowledgement.'

Elgar gave a derisive snort from where he was half hiding behind Grimm's bulk.

'Oh, there you are,' said Lucifer, fixing his gaze on the cat. 'Your family says hello, and your mother in particular is very irritated that you haven't written.'

'But . . .'

'And don't give me any of that tosh about being unable to hold a pen because you haven't got opposable thumbs. You're surrounded by be-thumbed people, why don't you ask one of them to draft a missive for you?'

'My family's alive?'

'Of course they're alive. Although your brother is a bit battered and bruised.'

'*What did you do to him?*' hissed Elgar, jumping onto the table and glaring at Lucifer.

A sharp intake of breath shot around the room. Jonathan glanced at Ignatius who looked like he was about to be sick.

'I,' said Lucifer, poking the end of Elgar's nose with his forefinger, 'have not done anything to your brother. A large bookcase fell on the poor lad and broke his leg. Would you like to know why?'

Elgar nodded dumbly, aware that all eyes were upon him.

'Your parents and brother have been working as archivists in my library. They were getting on splendidly until a week ago when, rather unexpectedly, an archdemon plummeted through the roof at high speed.'

'Oops!' winced Jonathan.

'Oops indeed,' said Lucifer. 'Still, it did have unintended – and, in my opinion, quite amusing – consequences. You gave me an excuse to deal with Belial once and for all. He broke the rules about not interfering in human affairs in such a public fashion that I couldn't just let him off with a bit of a dressing-down, could I?'

'What did you do to him?' asked Jonathan.

'I have his head mounted on a plaque over the fireplace, and his skin makes a fine hearthrug. Sorry you asked?'

Not knowing how to reply, Jonathan just stared.

'Anyway,' said Lucifer, 'in addition to paying my respects to Gabriel I wanted to see what all the fuss was about. I wanted to see . . . him.' He pointed at Jonathan.

'I take it you don't mean him any harm,' said Grimm, leaning forward. 'You even look at him funny and I'll—'

'You misunderstand me, my dear Halcyon,' said Lucifer, peering at the big man over the rim of his teacup. 'I rather like Jonathan; he's such an intriguing concept. Half-angel, half-demon, something that isn't supposed to be possible; and yet here he is. Slayer of archdemons, holder of memories, grandson of Gabriel and possessor of quite an interesting pair of wings apparently. What is it the Bible says about there being nothing new under the sun?'

Grimm sat back, but Jonathan could feel pressure building within him. His life had been torn apart by Belial, he was desperate to find his dad, and his mother had gone missing somewhere in Hell while trying to beg help from the very person now sitting across the table from him. Rather than offering assistance, Jonathan thought Lucifer appeared both hugely patronising and incredibly smug.

'*I've had enough!*' he suddenly shouted, surging to his feet as his wings burst into incandescent life. Everyone froze as imperial-purple ribbons of light filled the air around them. Slamming his fists to the table just in front of Elgar and making the cat jump out of his skin, Jonathan bellowed right into Lucifer's face, 'I'm not a museum exhibit. I don't care whether you think I'm interesting or not. Either help us or get the hell out!'

Lucifer jumped up too, leaning across the table until his face was close to Jonathan's. 'Why *should* I?' he shouted back. 'You're just a kid. You'll run screaming to Mummy at the first sign of trouble – that's if you knew where she *was*!'

Jonathan didn't know why he did it, but he didn't really care about the consequences at that point. Utterly furious, he pulled back his fist and punched Lucifer in the face. There was a muffled crack and Lucifer rocked back in his chair.

The atmosphere in the room instantly became so thick you could have spread it on toast. Jonathan looked about him at a ring of utterly horrified faces – Cay, in particular, looked as though she was about to pass out. Fully expecting Armageddon to restart in Sammael's living room, nobody dared breathe.

'That hurt,' groaned Lucifer, gingerly probing his nose with a finger and thumb. 'I think it's broken.'

His medical training taking over, Grimm got up, tipped Lucifer's head back, and with a practised hand swiftly repositioned the fallen angel's deviated septum. 'There you go,' he said. 'You'll probably want to put some ice on it.'

'I'll live,' said Lucifer, smiling at Jonathan.

'Um . . . sorry?' Jonathan offered by way of an apology.

'Not required,' replied Lucifer. 'Sorry for the goading, but I wanted to see what kind of fight you have inside you. I'm pleasantly surprised, I must say. I don't think anyone's broken my nose before – not even Sammael.'

Jonathan looked at his aunt. She had a hand over her mouth, but it looked like she was trying not to laugh.

'Creation doesn't need a shrinking violet, Jonathan,' said Lucifer. 'I have a feeling that you will need every ounce of determination you can muster if you and yours are to survive.'

'What do you mean?' asked Jonathan.

'You're an impossibility. You are a change in the order of things. I quite like that, but there are others who will not. Belial tried to use you, in a ham-fisted fashion, and even though he failed there has been . . . collateral damage, has there not?'

Jonathan nodded sadly.

'Baal and Lilith have been very quiet archdemons of late, but I have no desire to go to war with them because they think I've been interfering in the affairs of humanity. I came here today as I wished to pay my respects to your grandfather, and to see what kind of person you are. You may not believe me, but I would be . . . disappointed if anything too untoward were to happen to you.'

A thought suddenly occurred to Jonathan. 'Did Mum manage to find you?' he asked.

Lucifer shook his head. 'No. I'm afraid I haven't seen her. However, I will make some discreet enquiries. If she finds her way to my lands then I will send word to you, I promise.'

Jonathan's heart sank. If his mother hadn't made it to safety then there must be another reason for her absence, and it wasn't likely to be a pleasant one. Lucifer held out his hand and Jonathan shook it. He wasn't sure what to make of him, but the fallen angel sounded sincere.

'Right,' said Lucifer. 'I think I should take my leave. My apologies for disturbing your evening. I'll let myself out.' With a polite nod of his head, he left the way he had entered, gently closing the door behind him.

'I'm sorry,' said Elgar, after several moments' stunned silence from everyone.

'What for?' asked Sammael.

'For peeing on your chair. I've never been so frightened in my life. *Are you nuts?*' the cat shrieked at Jonathan. 'You broke the Devil's nose! What are you trying to do, start World War chuffin' Three in a windmill?'

'There was never any danger,' said Sammael softly.

'No danger?' Elgar ranted. 'Lucifer is the oldest and possibly the most powerful being in all of creation. He started a civil war that almost destroyed Heaven, and when that didn't work he came back with the three biggest, most psychotic archdemons he could find – *and their mates* – and tried to finish the job. And when he couldn't do that, he spent the next few centuries sulking. Not dangerous? It's like calling an active volcano slightly temperamental!' The cat finished his outburst and slumped panting to the table top, legs splayed out to all sides.

'Sammael is right, Elgar,' said Ignatius, running a hand through his hair. 'My own seat may be a trifle damp, but I don't think Lucifer meant us any harm. He deliberately tried to get under

Jonathan's skin to see how he would react. And don't forget that your family is safe and sound in Lucifer's castle.'

'Oh yeah,' huffed the cat. 'There is that.'

'Why didn't you think there was any danger, Sam?' asked Cay.

The angel sat down and took a sip of tea. 'There was no danger because I know something that nobody else does.'

'What?' asked Jonathan.

'Do you all promise to keep this to yourselves?' said Sammael, her face serious as she met the eyes of everyone present. They all nodded.

'Well, Lucifer isn't the being you think he is, not any more anyway. It would dent his quite substantial pride if what I'm about to tell you was common knowledge.'

'And what is this big secret?' said Elgar dismissively.

'Remember when I said that I fought Lucifer at Armageddon?'

'You beat him in single combat,' said Jonathan. 'Because of that you were able to stop the war between Heaven and Hell. If you hadn't there would have been nothing left to—' He paused, his eyes wide as an extraordinary thought popped into his head. 'You didn't *beat* Lucifer, did you?' he said to Sammael.

Everyone gasped in astonishment as the angel smiled and slowly shook her head. 'Smart boy. I was losing the fight, although only Lucifer knew that. So in order to save the creation he had helped to build he did the only thing he could do.'

'He let you win,' whispered Jonathan.

'Yes,' said Sammael. 'He swallowed his pride . . . and he let me win.'

Jonathan and Elgar walked Cay home across the green. It was very late, and the full moon was high in the night sky.

'Well, that was a day I won't forget in a hurry,' said the cat.

'Me neither,' said Jonathan. 'I'm glad your family is OK.'

'Yeah, that is such cool news,' grinned the cat. 'I even forgive you for breaking my brother's leg.'

'I didn't mean to,' said Jonathan. 'Thinking about it, maybe I should have dropped Belial somewhere else.'

'Nah,' said Elgar. 'I'm happy with the result. My brother gets his leg put in plaster and Belial gets stuffed and mounted. That's a fair trade-off in my book. I'm so filled with schadenfreude I might just burst.'

Jonathan turned to look at Cay. She had her face lifted towards the moon and she was smiling to herself. 'You OK?' he asked her. 'You've been very quiet today.'

'I'm fine,' she said as they arrived at the village shop.

Jonathan suddenly remembered something. 'When we were over at the vicarage this morning, you said you'd had a strange dream. We never got the chance to talk about it.'

'It'll keep,' said Cay. 'Anyway, you've got a big day tomorrow.'

Jonathan nodded. 'Yeah, I have.'

'G'nite, then. See you in the morning.'

'G'nite, Cay,' said Jonathan, watching his friend as she disappeared into her parents' cottage.

'Do you get the feeling there's something she's not telling us?' asked Elgar as they turned and walked back across the green to the vicarage. 'She was rather quick to change the subject away from strange dreams.'

'Hmm,' Jonathan pondered. 'There's something bothering her but there's no point giving her a hard time. She'll tell us when she's ready. Anyway, I need some sleep because tomorrow I'm going to do one thing, even if it kills me.'

'And that is?' asked Elgar.

'I'm going to rescue my dad.'

A Way In

Jonathan and Sammael sat next to each other by the edge of the pond. The village green was eerily quiet following a request from Ignatius that everyone keep away and let them work in peace. There was also the question of what might happen if something went wrong; Ignatius prayed that Sammael could cope with any incidents before Hobbes End got vaporised or sucked into another dimension.

'Do you think she knows what she's doing?' asked Elgar, sitting on the vicarage wall next to Montgomery, watching.

'I hope so,' said the gargoyle, 'but I don't know how she's going to open a gate without her wings. It's difficult enough to do it properly if you're at full strength. Gabriel rarely opened gates to anywhere – he said it was very dangerous.'

'Why is it dangerous?' asked Cay from where she stood in the vicarage gateway next to Ignatius and Grimm.

'Mr Stubbs?' said Montgomery, turning to his friend where he sat on his adjacent perch. 'You're the science expert. Please explain to Cay why ripping holes in the fabric of reality is fraught with peril.'

'Oh, all right then,' said Stubbs. 'If you must know, Cay, reality, time, space and all that is a bit like a giant carpet.'

'You mean you have to vacuum it once a week?' asked Elgar.

'No!' growled the gargoyle. 'I'm using a metaphor.'

'Oh, I see.'

'As I was saying . . . Gabriel told us that reality was like a carpet, woven together from all these threads of energy. He said that he and his siblings could use their wings to gently tease those threads apart, and open a doorway from one place to another. Jonathan did something similar when he dropped Belial on Lucifer's tower.'

'A good example, Mr Stubbs,' nodded Montgomery.

'So why is it fraught with peril?' asked Cay.

'Well, Gabriel said that every time a new gate was opened, however carefully, it damaged the weave of reality. I guess it's just like poking holes in a real carpet; eventually the whole lot will come apart.'

'That doesn't sound good,' said Cay.

'It isn't,' said Ignatius. 'Mr Stubbs is quite correct in his description. The risks involved are significant.'

'Didn't the Corvidae use a gate to take Jonathan's dad to Heaven in the first place?' asked Cay.

'Yeah,' said Stubbs. 'But that's a fixed point. It's always open. It's been there since the universe was created. Reality is riddled with them; it's like a Swiss cheese.'

'But we can't use *that* gate because the other end is deep inside Hell,' said Elgar. 'On the border between the domains of Belial and Baal. Belial may be gone but hordes of loyal demons from both camps will still be guarding the entry point. If Jonathan went all Rambo and tried to fight his way in, then he'd give Baal and Lilith all the excuse they need to kick off again. So if Jonathan wants to go to where the Corvidae left his dad, the best way to do it is for Sammael to open a portal between Hobbes End and the steps of Heaven. Jonathan could probably figure out how to do it himself in time, but I don't think he's in the mood to wait!'

'What's Heaven like?' Jonathan was asking Sammael, before she began her attempt.

The angel smiled. 'That's not an easy question to answer,' she said. 'It's not so much what it *looks* like but how it makes you *feel*. Yes, it's a vast city of white towers, delicate bridges and fountains carved from crystal, but they are just structures: they are not what truly makes Heaven. All the magnificent buildings, the wonderful boulevards, even the vast tree that grows at the centre are just things. It's what lies behind the façade that matters.'

'And what does lie behind it?' asked Jonathan.

'A song,' said Sammael. 'A simple hymn of joy to the glory of creation itself. It's etched into every stone. Every step you take echoes with it.' She shook her head and smiled. 'I'm not doing it justice, I'm afraid; you need to experience it for yourself. Hopefully, today will be our first step in getting you there. Now, I think I should begin.'

'Do you want me to help?' asked Jonathan.

'No,' replied Sammael. 'Just sit there and see if you can follow what I'm doing. If I make a mistake the consequences could be very unpleasant.'

Jonathan nodded; he had no desire to find out what Sammael classed as *unpleasant consequences*. He watched his aunt as she shut her eyes and began to breathe slowly and deeply, her hands placed flat on the ground in front of her. Minutes passed, but Jonathan couldn't sense anything happening. He was just about to ask Sammael if she was all right when she smiled and opened her eyes. 'Thank you,' she said.

'What for?'

'Not you, Jonathan; I was talking to Hobbes End. I just asked it if I could borrow Gabriel's power from where it lies beneath the waters of the pond.'

'It agreed, then?'

'Oh yes,' said Sammael. 'The village understands what I'm trying to do and it wants to help. I just need to—' She suddenly stopped speaking and gasped. Her eyes rolled back in her head and her fingers dug into the grass.

'Sam! Are you OK?' asked Jonathan, unsure if he should reach out and touch his aunt.

She nodded. 'I . . . had . . . forgotten,' she said, trying to compose herself.

'Forgotten what?'

'What it was like to have such raw power at my disposal. I didn't realise just how much of it Gabriel had given away either. This may be easier than I thought.'

Jonathan watched as his aunt got slowly to her feet, her eyes blazing silvery-blue. She tipped her head back and opened her arms wide as if welcoming a friend. For a moment nothing happened, then, from out of the ground at the angel's feet, ghostly ribbons of white light began to grow upward. More and more appeared until they formed a gently twisting column nearly three metres high.

The expression on her face one of utter joy, Sammael brought her palms together with a clap that echoed around the village like the tolling of a crystal bell. The column of ribbons parted, fanned out to the sides, reshaped itself into something magical.

And there, on the village green, Jonathan watched as the heart of Hobbes End gave itself form. The ribbons were thinner than his and the edges straight rather than serrated, but there was no mistaking the shape they made as they hung in the air. Jonathan knew that he was looking at a recreation of his grand-father's wings, given life by Sammael's will.

Gasps of astonishment burst from the villagers lining the road outside the vicarage. They had seen some incredible things over the years, some good, some terrifying, but watching Gabriel's legacy shining in front of them was overwhelming. Dancing in the sunlight, the wings radiated such happiness that it was impossible not to be moved.

'That is utterly marvellous,' said Grimm.

'Isn't it just,' whispered Ignatius.

Monty and Stubbs bounced up and down on their posts, excited beyond measure, while Cay and Elgar watched open-mouthed, basking in the sensation of almost having Gabriel back. The familiar scent of apples and beeswax flowed across the village and Cay's eyes filled with tears. The last time she had smelled that, Gabriel had sacrificed himself to save them all.

'And now the fun bit,' said Sammael. 'Watch with your head and your heart, Jonathan. Don't just see what I'm doing, *feel* it too.'

Jonathan nodded, his heart pounding in his chest. Finally, after weeks of waiting, he was able to start looking for his dad. He studied Sammael's hands as she began weaving them gently in the air. There was a pattern, but it was so complex that he could only catch tantalising glimpses of the whole. She was like a puppeteer putting a marionette through its paces.

The wing ribbons began to respond to her movements, arcane mathematics flowing within them. They fanned out, framing a rectangle the size of a large door. Sammael took a deep breath, held it and then, splaying her fingers, she slowly pushed her hands forward.

Jonathan's perception suddenly shifted. He was standing on the village green, but superimposed on this reality he saw a lattice of energy, pulsing with life. The tips of the wing ribbons shone like the sun as they gently slid into the centre of this lattice, took hold of the glowing threads, and with infinite care pulled the weave apart. Jonathan felt a soft breeze on his face as air rushed through the widening gate and into Hobbes End, equal-ising the pressure on both sides.

He watched in amazement as the world he knew was drawn

aside to reveal a scene of such contrast and wonder that he had trouble believing his eyes. He was still standing on the grass of the village green, but now looking at the entrance to Heaven through a door-shaped hole in reality. He turned to see the equally astonished faces of the inhabitants of Hobbes End. Ignatius seemed especially moved, and he wiped the corners of his eyes with the edge of his thumb.

Sammael gave a huge sigh and dropped her hands to her sides. 'Well, that went OK,' she said, smiling at Jonathan. 'I think the gate should hold; the village helped me enormously.'

'What do we do now?' asked Jonathan.

'We step through,' said Sammael. 'After you . . .' She gestured him forward.

Jonathan turned to face the gate. The edges rippled, but the disembodied wing ribbons seemed to be holding onto them securely. 'OK then,' he said. 'Let's do this.' With a backward glance towards the vicarage, he stepped out of a little village in the middle of an English forest – and into another world entirely.

Beneath his feet, a wide plaza of silver-veined marble spread out in all directions. Above him, bright constellations wheeled in a dark void so huge that it made his brain hurt to look at it for too long. And there, at the top of a flight of shallow steps were the gates that opened into Heaven proper. Impossibly tall and crafted from glass and gold, they were filled with an ever-lasting waterfall of quantum mathematics.

'It's just like I remember it,' Jonathan said to Sammael as she appeared at his side.

'How could you have seen this before?' she asked.

'It was when Gabriel died and gave me all his knowledge,' said Jonathan. 'For a while I was somewhere else, talking to my grandfather for the last time. He said we were standing in his memory of Heaven. He said that behind those gates I would see such wonders.'

'Ah, I see,' nodded Sammael. 'Well, he wasn't wrong. Let's get over there and see what we can find, shall we?'

'Yeah,' said Jonathan, striding off across the plaza with the angel at his side. As he walked towards the gates of Heaven he felt a growing sense of unease. He desperately wanted to save his father, but he wasn't sure if he could cope with finding his dead body lying slumped against that magnificent glass – a badly injured angel who had used the last of his strength to beat uselessly on a door that wouldn't open.

Unable to bear the waiting any longer, he broke into a run and vaulted up the steps two at a time. He came to a sudden halt at the top, unable to take his eyes from what he saw there.

Sammael arrived a moment later and stopped just as abruptly. 'Oh dear,' she said, placing a reassuring hand on Jonathan's shoulder.

In front of them, a horrible red-black stain spread out across the marble; there was so much of it that in places it had trickled down to the step below.

'It's *blood*,' said Jonathan. 'My father's blood. But where *is* he?'

'Look there,' said the angel. 'See how the blood thins out and becomes more of a wide smear? Someone opened Heaven's gates and dragged your father inside.'

Despite the awful evidence, hope welled up inside Jonathan. 'Then he may still be alive,' he whispered. 'Someone could be looking after him right now.'

'It's possible,' said Sammael.

'*Dad!*' Jonathan screamed out, stepping up to the gates and beating on them with his fist. '*Dad!*' The gates rang under his blows but they didn't budge. He felt something crunch under his feet, and looking down, he saw a cluster of small, black lumps, scattered across the white marble. He bent down and picked some up, cradling them in the palm of his hand; they left a grey-black smear on his skin. He took a careful sniff and was rewarded by the stench of burning.

'It's ash,' he said, turning his head to look at Sammael. 'Just like in my nightmare. My father's in danger and I need to get to him right now . . . *Dad!*' Furious and desperate, Jonathan refused to wait a moment longer. If nobody would let him in then he'd break the door down.

Before Sammael could stop him, Jonathan's wings sprang into life. With a scream of effort, he braced himself on his back foot and slammed the myriad ribbons into the gates of Heaven with every ounce of his strength.

'No. *Don't!*' Sammael cried out, but she was too late.

Jonathan's wings struck the gates with terrible force, and in an explosion of light and sound the gates struck back. His senses reeling, Jonathan felt himself lifted off his feet and thrown backwards down the steps to go skidding across the plaza. The ground heaved beneath him and at the back of his mind he heard a cry of pain. It took him a moment to realise that it was the village of Hobbes End that was screaming.

Raising his head, he could see Sammael clutching onto the side of the gate leading back to the village green. One of the edges had been ripped from the wing ribbons that held it open and creation was doing its best to mend the damage. The way home was rapidly closing and there was nothing the angel could do to stop it.

'*Jonathan!*' shouted Sammael. 'Get back through now!'

Jonathan clambered to his feet, but craned his head to look back at the entrance to Heaven as if he could open it by sheer force of will. 'Dad . . .' he sobbed.

'*For God's sake, boy, run!*' the angel bellowed at him, her face contorted with effort.

With all the speed he could muster, Jonathan stumbled towards his aunt and dived headfirst through the shrinking portal. As he did so he clipped Sammael's shoulder, ripping the edge of the gate from her hands. Thrown violently off balance, the angel fell heavily to the floor, her head hitting the marble with an awful crack.

Jonathan spun round and launched his wing ribbons towards Sammael, grabbing the angel around the waist and pulling her towards him. It was at that moment Hobbes End gave up the fight. The ghostly wings vanished and the ragged edges of the weave slammed shut like the jaws of a bear trap. It was only when his aunt fell to the ground next to him that Jonathan realised he had managed to get her through in one piece.

He kneeled down and brushed hair from the angel's face. 'Sam!' he cried out. 'Sam! Are you all right?'

The angel didn't answer. Her eyes were closed, her breathing was shallow, and a trickle of blood ran from her ear to stain the collar of her coat.

'Oh God, what have I done?' gasped Jonathan, putting a hand to his mouth in horror. '*What have I done?*'

Stairway to Heaven

Jonathan sat stunned as the inhabitants of Hobbes End ran forward to find out what had happened. Grimm kneeled by Sammael and began to examine her with practised hands while Ignatius gripped Jonathan's shoulders.

'Did something go wrong?' he asked. 'Why did you come back so quickly? What was that huge bang we all heard?'

'It . . . it was my fault,' said Jonathan. 'I lost my temper. I was so angry that the gates of Heaven wouldn't open that I hit them, Ignatius. I hit them with my wings and they didn't like it. They reflected my attack back at me. That was the bang you heard. Hobbes End lost control of the gate back to here and it started to close. Sammael held it open as long as she could so I had time to get through, but she fell and hit her head. I only just managed to pull her after me; I'm so stupid.'

Ignatius heaved a sigh and patted Jonathan on the shoulder. 'We all make mistakes,' he said. 'You just wanted to find your dad so badly you did something daft; it's understandable.'

'Yeah, but what about Sam?'

'Grimm?' asked Ignatius. 'How is she?'

Grimm frowned. 'I'm no expert on the anatomy of angels, but I'd say she was out cold and is likely to have a concussion. She'll live, but she'll have a prize-winning headache.'

Jonathan gasped with relief. 'Thank you, Grimm.'

'Don't thank me,' said the big man. 'Thank angelic constitution. I tell you, Jonathan, whatever you did up there, please don't do it again!'

'I won't, Grimm,' promised Jonathan. 'I'm so sorry.'

'No point crying over spilt milk, lad. What did you find anyway?'

'I saw where the Corvidae left my dad. And . . . there was so much blood. But someone must have opened Heaven's gates and taken Dad inside because there were these drag marks. They reminded me so much of when the Corvidae took Gabriel.'

Ignatius and Grimm looked at each other. They both remembered the awful stains where Gabriel had been dragged from his cottage during his kidnapping by Rook, Raven and Crow.

'Oh, my boy,' said Ignatius.

'But that wasn't all,' said Jonathan. 'Scattered on the ground was this carpet of ash. It was just like my nightmare. What if Raphael has really gone mad with grief and destroyed Heaven? What if my dad is in there, dying, with nobody to help him but a mad archangel?'

Ignatius took a deep breath. 'That is a frightening thought, Jonathan,' he said. 'But right now, we need to go and make sure Sammael is OK. Grimm and I will take her to the windmill and sit with her until she wakes up. Will you be all right until then?'

'Yeah,' sighed Jonathan. 'With the gates of Heaven locked

shut, there's no way I can get in until I figure out how to use this.' He waved his wristwatch at Ignatius.

'I know,' said the vicar. 'But don't push yourself. The more desperate you get, the more mistakes you will make. Wait until Sammael wakes up and talk to her, ask her advice about what to do next.'

Jonathan nodded, but deep down he was afraid that his aunt wouldn't be particularly helpful. He had almost got her killed just now, after all.

Cay and Elgar came to sit with him as the crowd dispersed. 'Are you OK?' Cay asked.

Jonathan shook his head. 'I messed up big time,' he said. 'I'll be lucky if Sam ever talks to me again.'

'Of course she will,' said Cay. 'You're her family.'

'I got angry and this is the result,' said Jonathan. 'I can't risk anybody else getting hurt because of me. Anyway, I know where Dad is now, so all I have to do is figure out how to get to him.'

'But don't you want to wait for Sammael?' asked Cay.

'I can't,' said Jonathan. 'I need to go now. There is something really wrong inside Heaven and Dad is stuck there in the middle of it. There's only one way to figure out how to use this watch – I'm going to go back into that library in my head and ask it to help me!'

'You have absolutely no idea what you're doing!' said Elgar as both he and Cay followed Jonathan to the remains of Gabriel's cottage.

'Maybe not,' said Jonathan. 'But I'm not just going to sit and wait. Dad is relying on me or he wouldn't have appeared in my nightmare.'

'What if it wasn't your dad?' asked Cay.

'Who else would it be?' retorted Jonathan. 'Belial and the Corvidae are dead and gone, and Lucifer said that Baal and Lilith are just keeping themselves to themselves.'

'What Lucifer actually said was that they had been very quiet,' said Elgar. 'It's not the same thing.'

'I don't care!' said Jonathan. 'I'm going to find a way into Heaven and that's final. I know that Gabriel placed a back door in his old workshop; what I don't know is where the entry point is here in Hobbes End.'

'My guess is that it's the cupboard door in his cottage, the one we used to go and find the Clock in the first place,' suggested Elgar.

'But the cottage is a pile of rubble,' sighed Jonathan, his shoulders sagging in frustration. 'Won't this end of the gate have been destroyed?'

'I doubt it,' said Elgar. 'How do you destroy something that's not actually there until you use it?'

'Good point,' said Jonathan.

'Please don't do this,' begged Cay. 'Anything could be on the other side of that gate.'

'I know,' said Jonathan, giving Cay's hand a squeeze. 'But what would you do if it was your mum or dad trapped in there?'

'I'd try to get to them,' she sighed.

'Exactly. So help me with this, please, Cay. Don't try to stop me.'

She nodded, but deep down Cay knew that something was not as it seemed. She couldn't explain why, but her senses were becoming more acute by the day and something about Jonathan's desire to get into Heaven just didn't *smell* right. She so wanted to tell Jonathan about her dream – about what she was becoming – but she knew that what he wanted most was to find his parents. She would share her secret with him when he had time to think about something else but his search.

'So what now?' asked Elgar.

'Now I go and check out a library book,' said Jonathan, sitting down and closing his eyes. It took a while for him to relax; his heart was still beating fast and he knew that if he didn't manage to centre himself then he'd get nowhere. Taking a deep breath, he willed himself to be calm and still, to see that vast repository of information inside his head.

Soon, just as he had when he'd fixed Stubbs's ear, Jonathan felt himself in two places at once. He could feel the breeze on his face, smell the grass of the churchyard, but around him he could see the library housing all his grandfather's knowledge.

Not wanting to waste any time, he sat at the reading table and took off his watch. Holding Gabriel's Clock in his hand, he tried to imagine what his grandfather would have been thinking when he designed it. What would be the trigger? Would it be simple or complex; would it activate with a thought or with a spoken word?

There was a sudden change in the library's atmosphere, and Jonathan looked up to see something that almost made him jump out of his skin. Sitting opposite him was the translucent figure of an elderly man, also holding a watch in his hands. It was his grandfather; it was Gabriel.

Jonathan opened his mouth to speak but realised it would be pointless. This wasn't his grandfather's ghost or his soul, or anything sentient. There was an absence to the apparition, and Jonathan felt the all-too-familiar ache of loss in his heart as he realised this was just a recording of sorts. A message left for him by his grandfather, to be accessed once he had the understanding to request it.

Jonathan stood up and walked round the table to stand next to Gabriel. He knew that if he reached out his hand it would pass right through the archangel's image, but he refrained from doing so. It seemed disrespectful somehow. On the table in front of Gabriel was a blueprint covered in notes, diagrams and scribbles. It was obvious to Jonathan that the blueprint was for the watch that he held in his hand.

Without warning the image began to move, and the ghostlike Gabriel ran his finger underneath a row of six numbers written on the blueprint. He then proceeded to delicately rotate the knurled winder on the side of the watch so the numbers appearing in the date window followed the same order as those that were written down. Each time a number matched up, Gabriel pressed the winder until it clicked. Once the sequence had been entered, the image of the seated angel flickered and he repeated his actions,

'It can't be that simple,' Jonathan gasped. 'It can't be!'

'What can't be?' asked Cay.

Jonathan shook his head, disorientated from suddenly being back in the churchyard. 'The answer,' he said, unable to keep a smile from his face. 'I know how to use Gabriel's Clock. I can get into Heaven. Watch this.'

Cay and Elgar stared as Jonathan took off his wristwatch and copied his grandfather's actions.

'What are you doing?' asked Cay

'Entering the right combination,' said Jonathan.

'And that would be . . . ?' asked Elgar.

'A day, a month and a year,' said Jonathan. 'The date I was born.'

The air around them suddenly filled with a low hum, and the remains of the cottage began to shake. Sparks of static crackled across every surface and Elgar yowled in alarm as his fur stood on end. High above the rubble, a hole in reality shaped just like the door that used to be in Gabriel's attic slowly materialised. It was edged with a thin strip of blue light and just hung there in space, completely unsupported.

'Well, that looks familiar,' said Elgar. 'Do you think it leads into Heaven?'

'There's only one way to find out,' said Jonathan. 'I think there's a ladder lying against the rear of the church. Grimm was using it to clean the windows the other day. Come and give me a hand, Cay.'

'Are you sure about this?' she asked, her face worried.

'Yeah,' said Jonathan. 'I know enough to look after myself, and I really don't want anyone else getting hurt.'

'I'll come!' offered Elgar. 'I can be the first demon to visit Heaven. You can carry me through the gate just like you did when we went looking for the Clock.'

'Sorry, cat,' said Jonathan. 'It's just too risky. I couldn't handle it if anything happened to you. You know where your family is now and you need to keep yourself in one piece so you can go and see them.' He reached down to stroke Elgar's head. 'We'll have plenty of chances for other adventures together, just not today.'

'OK,' said Elgar. 'I suppose you're right. Aren't you going to let anyone else know what you're doing, though? Ignatius and Grimm will be really upset once they find out that you've gone.'

'I know,' said Jonathan. 'But they've already risked everything for me and they have to look after Sammael. It's time for me to show I can sort out my own problems.'

'But—' Cay began.

'Please, Cay,' begged Jonathan. 'Just let me do this. Let me go and save Dad.'

She looked at him sadly. 'OK,' she said. 'We'll tell Ignatius where you've gone.'

'Thank you,' he said. 'Now, give me a hand with the ladder.'

They carried it back to the remains of Gabriel's cottage, and after clambering up the pile of rubble, managed to rest the top of the ladder against the edge of the blue-rimmed door.

'How come you don't just fly up?' asked Elgar.

'I still can't figure out how flying works,' said Jonathan. 'When I fought Belial, Gabriel was with me and he did all the difficult stuff. There's so much for me to learn it's hard to know where to start.'

'Fair enough,' said the cat. 'Well then, I guess this is it. Please don't get killed – think of the paperwork.'

'I'll try not to,' said Jonathan.

'Come back safe,' said Cay, throwing her arms around his neck and giving him a hug.

Jonathan smiled. 'I will,' he said. He turned to look at the ladder and put a foot on the first rung. 'I'm coming for you, Dad,' he said under his breath. 'I'm coming.'

And before he had time to feel afraid, he climbed up to the gate and stepped into Heaven itself.

Silent Running

'*He's done what?*' shouted Ignatius, a look of horror on his face.

'All right, all right, keep your dog collar on!' said Elgar. 'Don't shoot the messenger. It's not Cay's fault. Jonathan finally figured out how to use Gabriel's Clock and wanted to go get his dad without anyone else getting hurt, especially after the accident with Sammael.'

'What's going on?' asked Grimm, coming down the stairs that led to the upper floors of the windmill.

'Jonathan figured how to use Gabriel's Clock and decided to sneak into Heaven without any backup,' sighed Ignatius. 'I know he's desperate to get to his dad but he needed to wait for Sammael. She would have been able to help him.'

'But isn't Sam badly injured?' asked Cay.

'Yes,' said Grimm. 'She's unconscious, but she's still an arch-angel; she'll be as right as rain in a day or so.'

'Oh,' said Cay, wondering if she should have done more to stop Jonathan.

'Don't blame yourself,' said Ignatius. 'You wouldn't have been able to stop him anyway. None of us could, to be honest. We just have to hope that there's nothing nasty waiting for him, or if there is, that he's powerful enough to deal with it.'

'OK,' sighed Cay, knowing that what Ignatius said was true, but still wishing she had said or done something at least to make Jonathan stay in Hobbes End a little longer. Leaving the windmill with Elgar at her heels, she started walking home, her shoulders slumping more and more with each step she took.

'There's nothing you could have done to stop him,' said Elgar. 'You need to let Jonathan make his own mistakes, assuming that he *has* made one, of course. It might be that he pops back home at dinner time with his dad in tow.'

'I know,' said Cay. 'I'm just fed up not being able to help. I'm just a kid, I'm not a superhero.'

Elgar paused before answering. 'I think you know that's not entirely true,' he said, grinning.

'What do you mean?'

'I mean that you're not as useless as you like to make out,' said the cat. 'You're forgetting that I have a particularly good nose for these things. You don't smell the same as you did a week ago.'

'You're making it up,' said Cay, a defensive edge creeping into her voice.

'I don't think so,' said Elgar. 'How does that fairy tale go, the one with the pigs and the big bad wolf? I'll huff and I'll puff and I'll—'

'OK! So I'm a werewolf! Just like Dad. You happy now?' Cay snapped.

'Of course I'm happy,' said the grinning cat. 'What's not to like? You finally get to be who you were always meant to be. How can that not be a good thing?'

'I thought you'd make fun of me!' said Cay.

'Of course I'm going to make fun of you,' said Elgar. 'But I'd do that anyway. Especially if you became a werebadger – that'd be hilarious. It'd be like the *Twilight* books meeting *Wind in the Willows*.'

Cay couldn't help but chuckle to herself. It was good that some things never seemed to change, and Elgar was top of that list.

'Your dad's waiting for you,' said the cat.

Cay looked up and saw her father standing outside the shop and waving to her. He had a blanket over his arm.

'I wonder what he wants?' said Cay.

'Let's go and find out,' said Elgar.

They ran over to Kenneth Forrester and he smiled broadly at them both.

'Hi, Dad,' said Cay. 'What's up?'

'I thought it was time we went for a run together,' he said. 'Your mother's waiting out back.'

'You mean . . . ?'

Kenneth nodded. 'The sooner you try, the sooner you'll adjust. I take it Elgar has already figured out what's happening, given the huge grin on his face?'

'I've known for a week,' said the cat.

'Do you have any objection to him coming along?' Kenneth asked his daughter.

Cay looked at Elgar. 'No,' she said. 'He's my friend, and I have nothing to be ashamed of.'

'Good answer,' said Mr Forrester. 'Let's go, shall we?'

In a secluded glade deep within the forest, Cay lay on a soft bank of mossy ground. She was wrapped loosely in the blanket her father had brought with him in order to protect her modesty.

'That's the one irritating thing about being a shapechanger,' he'd said to Cay on their walk to the glade. 'You have to take your clothes off before you change if you don't want them ripped to pieces. There's also the fact that a wolf in boxer shorts looks ridiculous.'

Cay knew that what her father was saying was completely true, but lying here under the forest canopy, naked except for a blanket and with her parents and Elgar watching her, she felt really weird. 'What do I do?' she asked her father as he kneeled next to her and gently stroked her hair.

'Nothing,' he said. 'Just smell the forest around you. Look at the way the sunlight filters through the leaves; see the birds as they perch on branches and fly to their nests. Watch the creepy crawlies as they scurry across the ground. You've got ants and woodlice, beetles and spiders. All around us are rabbits and deer and pheasants, each doing their own thing. All of them belong here; this is their home. It's your home too when you're a wolf. I know you've been dreaming of this, so it's time to let the dream meet the day. Don't be afraid, daughter – become something even more wonderful than you already are.'

Cay felt herself lulled into a half-sleep by her father's deep, rumbling voice. She forgot about everything that had been bothering her and extended her senses into the forest. It thrummed with life and her heartbeat quickened to meet it. Every living thing had its own halo, just as she had dreamed.

The blanket became too confining, so she shrugged it off and got to her feet, sniffing the air about her. She could smell the water of the lake a mile to the north, and someone in the village had a bonfire in their garden. Her hearing was extraordinary too; she could hear Angus McFadden's car as he drove home along the forest road. She knew the car belonged to Angus because of the way the engine sounded. Underneath it all was a sense of the village and the forest that surrounded it being more alive than Cay had dreamed possible. Apples and beeswax mixed with hope and constancy, untouched and untouchable by the world outside.

Placing one paw in front of the other Cay began to run, revelling in the ease with which her legs propelled her forward. This is wonderful, she thought as the undergrowth flashed past. She increased her speed, and for long moments she was entirely airborne. *Can you see me, Gabriel?* she asked the air. *I don't have wings but I'm flying, in my own way.*

She looked to her left and saw that a huge, black-and-silver wolf had joined her, matching her speed without effort. The wolf reached out with his muzzle and nudged Cay affectionately behind her pointed ears.

Hello, Dad, she said to herself. The huge wolf gave a joyful howl and launched himself off toward the lake, and his daughter, her red fur glowing like embers in the dappled sunlight, followed him.

Elgar and Joanne Forrester sat next to each other on the trunk of a fallen ash tree and watched the two wolves disappear into the forest.

Elgar turned to Joanne only to see tears running down her face. She was smiling, but she was obviously upset. Elgar nudged her arm with his nose to get her attention.

'What's the matter?' he asked, speaking slowly so she could read his lips.

Mrs Forrester took a small notebook from her coat pocket and wrote something before showing it to Elgar.

My husband and daughter are beautiful, said the note.

'Then why are you unhappy?' asked Elgar.

Because I would love to join them and I can't, wrote Joanne.

'Oh, I see,' said Elgar. 'I understand that. It's tough when you would like to be something other than what you are.'

And do you wish to be something else?

'I miss my family,' said Elgar. 'I'm stuck in the shape of a cat – which I admit is huge fun most of the time – but this isn't really who I am. Anyway, with Belial dead there's no way to lift his curse. A cat I shall have to stay.'

Mrs Forrester picked Elgar up and sat him on her lap. *Then we shall yearn to be different together*, she wrote.

Elgar nodded. 'Yeah, Mrs F,' he said. 'That we shall.'

Happy in each other's company, cat and woman waited in the quiet of the forest for the wolves of Hobbes End to finish their run and come home.

Ashes to Ashes

Jonathan stared at his cramped and dusty surroundings; he was in a small room, not much more than a cupboard. The walls and floor were bare stone, and in front of him a sturdy wooden door led onward. Trying to be as quiet as possible, Jonathan walked over and tried the handle of the door. It wasn't locked, so he opened it just a crack to see what lay beyond.

What he saw made him gasp in astonishment. When Gabriel had mentioned his workshop in Heaven, Jonathan had always thought of a modest room with a forge and tools. The truth was radically different. On the other side of the door was a space the size of an aircraft hangar, its roof and walls made from panels of translucent glass supported by a delicate framework of metal struts. The floor was littered with sturdy wooden benches – each one shrouded in a dust sheet – and against the walls stood ranks of silent machines, their purpose a mystery. Half-finished contraptions floated in mid-air, cradled by heavy chains that dangled from the ceiling, while a pale grey light filtered in from outside, lending a melancholy air to the work Gabriel had left behind. The silence was absolute, and dust lay thick on every surface.

Deciding that it was safe to proceed, Jonathan stepped into the room and gently shut the door behind him, marking its location in case he had to make a run for it. He began walking between two rows of benches, and he'd gone some distance when he realised that somehow he knew where he was going. In the far corner of the workshop there would be a side door that opened onto a small, walled garden – a garden in which Gabriel had loved to sit when he'd needed to rest.

'How do I know that?' Jonathan asked himself. But as soon as the question passed his lips he knew the answer. Amid all that knowledge he'd inherited from his grandfather were memories. Not picture-perfect recollections, but a tangled bundle made from sight and sound, touch and smell, happy and sad. Jonathan knew that his grandfather had been at his happiest right here in this huge room, fixing the unfixable before taking a book outside to sit on the grass and read. It was here that Gabriel's memories were so strong that Jonathan could almost see Heaven through his grandfather's eyes.

'I like it here too, Gabriel,' he said, meaning every word. There was something about the unfinished work on all sides that called to Jonathan. He didn't like it nowadays when something was broken – he had a growing desire to mend things, to bring matters to a satisfactory conclusion.

He continued his walk, eventually reaching a space in the centre of the workshop where the benches had been pushed aside to accommodate a huge mound hidden beneath a sheet. Unable to restrain his curiosity, Jonathan grabbed the edge of the sheet and pulled carefully. The dust sheet flowed to the workshop floor in a rippling wave of cotton as dust exploded outward in all directions. Coughing, sneezing and half-blind, Jonathan waited for the cloud to settle before wiping his eyes on his sleeve and staring in amazement at what lay before him.

There, curled up on the stone floor as if asleep, was Brass, or rather a construct that at first glance looked a lot like Brass. Closer inspection revealed some obvious differences, however. There was something rudimentary about this dragon's construction; it just wasn't as . . . Jonathan struggled for the right word . . . as *graceful* as the version sleeping at the bottom of the village pond.

'You're a prototype, aren't you, girl?' said Jonathan as he walked round the motionless dragon, letting the tips of his fingers brush the unpolished metal. 'Maybe even the very first, given the others we saw when went to find the Clock. How long have you been here I wonder?'

The dragon remained unresponsive, no life evident in its skeletal, unfinished frame.

Jonathan heaved a sigh and reluctantly continued on his way. He had more important matters to focus on, but there was something sad about the abandoned construct. Maybe I could finish it one day? he thought. Trudging onward across the dusty floor, he gradually felt a sense of unease creep over him. At first he couldn't tell why, but the more he thought about it the more he realised that something about the workshop wasn't quite right.

'It's too dark,' he said out loud as Gabriel's memories showed him that the workshop should be full of light: a gleaming palace of wonders encased in a crystal shell. 'Heaven is powered by the sun, night never falls, so why is the light coming in from outside so grey and weak?' Trying hard not to worry, he continued on his way.

He rounded the corner of a line of benches and suddenly there it was: a door he'd never seen, but yet he knew as intimately as the lines on the palm of his hand. It was small and plain, built from oak, with brass hinges, secured with a simple latch. Jonathan walked up to it, lifted the metal bar and placed his hand on the smooth timber to give the door a push. As he did so, he saw the ghost of Gabriel's hand superimposed on his, performing the same action. 'How many times did you open this door, Grandfather?' Jonathan whispered, feeling sad to be so close to where Gabriel had spent most of his life, yet only having fleeting memories of the angel for comfort.

He shook his head. He was getting distracted by the past; he was here to find his father and he needed to get on with his search. He pushed the door, fully expecting it to swing open with little effort. It moved slightly, but then came to a sudden stop.

Jonathan frowned and the sick feeling in the pit of his stomach grew. Realising that he had no option if he was to see what was outside, he put his shoulder to the wood, braced his feet and pushed as firmly and as carefully as he could. The door resisted for a moment, then opened with a scraping noise that set

Jonathan's teeth on edge. In the all-enveloping silence, the noise of the door as it moved seemed incredibly loud. Jonathan winced, but continued pushing until there was enough space to slip through the gap. He took one last look over his shoulder at the shrouded secrets lying dormant in the workshop, then made his way outside and into the walled garden where his grandfather had loved to sit.

It was the smell that hit him first. The acrid reek of ash hung in the air and lingering wisps of smoke stung his eyes. What light there was filtered down through roiling grey clouds that scudded across the sky, even though there wasn't a breath of wind. The awful truth of Jonathan's nightmare hit him full in the face. What greenery had once filled the garden had been incinerated; beneath his feet, lush grass had been reduced to a carpet of cinders.

'Oh no . . .' he cried softly. 'Please, no! It was just a bad dream.'

Through the murk he could see an archway in the garden wall, and with faltering steps he walked across the ruined lawn to peer through it. At long last he was gazing upon Heaven, and what he saw made him drop to his knees. Tears streamed down his face and dropped silently into the thirsty ash as he looked about him in shocked incomprehension.

Jonathan had hoped to see creation in all its glory, a place of wonder as Sammael had described it, the home of his father and grandfather. Instead, he was faced with utter destruction. On all sides lay the shattered ruins of a once-magnificent city. Scorched stone, twisted metal and clouds of slowly drifting smoke filled his sight. In the distance, at the end of a wide and strangely familiar boulevard, stood the burnt trunk of a huge tree, its bare and blasted branches reaching towards an unforgiving sky as if begging for help.

Jonathan shut his eyes, as though by denying what he saw he could change the terrible existence of such carnage. Inside his head, images of the way Heaven *had* been flashed up one after another, the contrast between the past and present awful beyond words. If memories could cry, Jonathan knew that his grandfather would be weeping.

He slumped forward, and as he did so he felt something crunch beneath the palms of his hands. He looked down and realised with mounting horror that his nightmare wasn't fantasy. It was more real than he would have believed possible. In all directions, as far as he could see, bones lay half buried. Jonathan clamped a filthy hand to his mouth to stop himself from screaming.

The seconds ticked by, and he managed to collect himself enough to get to his feet. He had dreamed this, and now he was standing in the cold ashes of the aftermath, a brutal truth that was impossible to ignore. He had hoped to find someone who might know what had happened to his father, but now he realised that he was utterly alone and he wasn't sure what to do next.

The thought of going back to Hobbes End with empty hands and such awful news was not an option, so Jonathan decided to explore the remains of the city as best he could.

With no idea where he should start, he began walking down

the wide boulevard towards the huge tree; it loomed over the devastation like a gnarled hand trying to dig itself out of a grave. Silence reigned, but the sensation of being watched from the blackened and empty windows all about him began to grow.

'Don't be daft,' he said aloud, taking comfort in hearing the sound of his own voice. 'There's nobody there. Just keep moving. Try and find the gates, see if there's any sign of Dad just inside there.'

Nodding with agreement at his own idea he continued on his way. It was only when he'd been walking for several minutes that he realised how big the tree that he was heading for must be. The boulevard stretched on into the distance, and the tree grew and grew until it almost filled the sky. Most of the branches jutted out from the main trunk far above the ground, but there were some lower down, and it was one of these branches that made Jonathan stop dead in his tracks.

He'd thought he'd seen the limit of the violence visited upon Heaven, but with growing despair he realised that he was wrong. A rope was lashed to the lowest branch of the tree and at its end dangled a man's body. The rope was looped about his neck in a noose, and his head hung forward onto his chest, obscuring his features.

'Oh no!' cried Jonathan, breaking into a run. 'Please don't let it be—' He didn't want to finish the sentence; some things were just too terrible to contemplate. The last few steps were agony, but Jonathan finally stood beneath the great tree and could look upward into the hanged man's face. Mercifully it wasn't his father, but the features were familiar, not to him, but to Gabriel's memories.

Gabriel knew the face that dangled from the end of that rope; he'd grown up with him, worked with him, fought by his side and loved him. The face belonged to Gabriel's brother, Raphael Executor, and it radiated such despair that Jonathan could do nothing but sink back to his knees in the dust.

No corruption had touched the archangel's corpse. It was as if his despair was so great that even death would not properly claim him. Jonathan stared at Raphael and felt an ache in his chest that dwarfed anything he'd ever felt before. It was as if the destruction of Heaven was mirrored in the contours of Raphael's face.

'Do not let it claim you too, my son,' said a warm voice, the speaker placing a firm hand on Jonathan's shoulder. 'Raphael's despair must not become your burden.'

Jonathan shut his eyes, but couldn't stop the tears that ran from them. He knew that voice as well as his own. 'Are you real?' he asked, unwilling to turn round in case his mind was playing tricks on him. The hand on his shoulder gave him a squeeze, and Jonathan reached his own hand up to meet it. He felt himself lifted to his feet by two strong arms which then enveloped him in a huge hug. The familiar smell of the man overwhelmed him and Jonathan let out a cry that he'd been holding inside him for weeks.

'My son,' said the man, kissing the top of Jonathan's head.

'Oh, Dad,' said Jonathan, wrapping his arms around his father

117

and squeezing him as hard as he possibly could. For one glorious moment as Jonathan and his father stood amid destruction on a cataclysmic scale, everything was all right.

A Perfect Prison

Jonathan looked at his father and smiled, almost unwilling to believe his eyes. 'It's you, isn't it?' he asked.

'It's me,' said Darriel. 'I'm so sorry you had to see all this. You weren't supposed to come and find me.'

'But why?'

'Because it's what the archdemon Baal wanted you to do,' said Darriel. 'Your nightmare didn't come from me. It was sent by him.'

'But you were hurt – you and that boy angel asked me to come and save you.'

Darriel shook his head. 'I was in your dream,' he said. 'But I wasn't the phantom holding that false child's hand, I was the burning angel who grabbed your leg and told you to stay away.'

'I don't understand,' said Jonathan.

'Baal,' said Darriel. 'He caused all this. He was the one who sent you the message to come here, the one disguised as a boy angel. He used an image of me to lure you here. I knew what he was doing and tried to stop him, but he was too strong. He made me look like a burned corpse so you'd be frightened of me.'

Jonathan thought back to his nightmare and knew that what his father was telling him was true. The burned angel that had grabbed his ankle may have looked horrific, but he had bright blue eyes, just like his own.

'But why did you want me to stay away?' asked Jonathan. 'You're hurt, aren't you? Why wouldn't you want me to come and take you back to Hobbes End?'

Darriel looked at his son and sighed. 'Because this is a trap,' he said. 'I don't know how you managed to get into Heaven but you need to leave right now! Baal is coming.'

'What does Baal want?' asked Jonathan. 'Why would he set a trap for me?'

Darriel shook his head. 'Please, you need to get out of here,' he begged.

'Then let's go before Baal arrives!' cried Jonathan. 'Come back with me to Hobbes End. There's a secret gate in Gabriel's workshop that we can use.'

'So that's how you managed it,' said Darriel. 'My father was always full of surprises. I guess Baal must have known you would use it to get into Heaven sooner or later.'

Jonathan frowned. 'I guess news travels fast in Hell. Baal could have found out about the back door to Heaven in any number of ways.'

Darriel nodded, but his face was sad.

'What is it?' asked Jonathan.

'I want to come with you, son, but I can't. I'm stuck here.'

'What do you mean you're stuck here?'

'It'll take too long to explain. You need to go.'

'I'm not leaving until you tell me what's going on,' said Jonathan. 'Ever since the Corvidae attacked us I've been running. You didn't tell me anything that I needed to know. I didn't know what I was, who I was. Grandfather sacrificed himself to save me!'

Darriel hung his head. 'I know,' he whispered. 'I felt him die.'

'He was so worried about you, Dad,' said Jonathan.

'Belial hurt me . . . badly,' sighed Darriel.

'But you're OK, aren't you?'

Darriel nodded. 'I had . . . help, but you need to go, son. And I cannot leave with you.'

'I don't believe you,' said Jonathan. 'Help me understand; tell me what happened here.'

Darriel was silent for a moment. 'Very well; if it means that you'll listen. Reach out and touch Raphael, let him tell you the story of what happened here. He is still suffering, frozen in time at the moment of his death, waiting for someone to give him absolution for his crimes, waiting to tell someone the truth.'

'What do you mean?' asked Jonathan.

'Just touch him,' said Darriel. 'He can show you much better than I.'

Jonathan hesitantly reached out to touch the body of the hanged archangel. As soon as his fingers brushed the hem of Raphael's robe, he felt as though he'd been struck hard across the face. His legs sagged but he found himself unable to let go.

A flood of terrible imagery drove itself into his mind; unable to look away, Jonathan learned of Heaven's fate.

Once again he was at the battle of Armageddon. He'd seen it from Gabriel and Sammael's point of view, but now he saw it through Raphael's eyes. He felt his heart break as he cradled the dying Bethesda in his lap, felt his passion for life ebb away with the diminishing beat of his beloved's heart. He despaired, and that was the beginning of the end.

Jonathan saw Raphael return to Heaven as a broken angel, nursing a grudge against Sammael for not using the Cherubim to wipe out Lucifer and the demon horde. Locked away in his tower, Raphael retreated from his duties until one day a young boy angel returned to Heaven, part of a group of survivors from the battle with Hell. The young boy crept unnoticed into Raphael's tower and whispered in his ear while he slept, building on the despair already filling the angel's heart.

By the time he awoke, Raphael was completely under the control of the boy angel. Doing his new master's bidding, his first act was to send the archangel Michael rushing to Sammael's aid just as she ignited her last star. Flying from Heaven at full speed, Michael tore open a gate to the location Raphael had given him just as the star sprang into life. Michael was incinerated and Sammael, racked with guilt at killing her brother, let Raphael exile her.

Remaining in the shadows, the boy angel continued to whisper poison into Raphael's ear, driving him further and further into madness. Eventually even Gabriel – bereft at the loss of Sammael and Michael – exiled himself, leaving an insane archangel in sole control of Heaven. It was not long before the boy angel decided that it was time for an end to his deception.

Raphael walked with his new companion to the gates of Heaven, and using the glass-bladed sword of office forged for him by Sammael, he sealed the gates shut.

'Burn this place to the ground,' the boy angel said. 'It has been infiltrated by demons. The war is not over, Raphael. You are the only one who can stop them. Show them no mercy; remember your beloved!'

In his broken mind Raphael saw only what the boy wanted him to see. His home, he believed, was infested with creatures like those that had killed Bethesda. Rage filled the archangel, and manifesting his wings he unleashed hell on a tired, scared and unsuspecting population until he was too weak to stand. Fire rained from the sky, and a wall of flame swept along the boulevard, incinerating everything in its path. The only way out was the locked door behind Raphael.

Nobody had stood a chance. Stone shattered in the heat, the sky filled with smoke, and the tree at the centre of Heaven – the oldest thing in all of creation apart from Lucifer – burned. It was all over within minutes. Every man, woman and child in Heaven died at Raphael's hand.

Pleased that he had apparently killed the enemy, Raphael allowed the boy angel to lead him along the smoking boulevard to the base of the great tree. Once there, the boy tied a noose around the Raphael's neck and threw the other end of the rope he carried over the lowest branch.

'What are you doing?' Raphael asked.

'Tying up loose ends,' said the boy, before whispering in Raphael's ear one last, awful time. With delight bordering on the obscene, the boy removed his spell from Raphael and let him see the truth of what he had done.

The archangel looked on aghast at the destruction he had caused, so far beyond horror that he could do nothing except stand and weep, too exhausted to even call upon his wings.

The boy had crowed in Raphael's face then. 'I am Baal, you fool! This body is nothing but a construct the likes of which your brother is so fond of making. My soul sits inside it, safe from detection, a perfect disguise in which to walk into Heaven and trick you into destroying everything you have ever loved. Your pathetic weakness at the loss of Bethesda gave me all the opening I needed. I am the archdemon of despair, and today I have fed so very well. Goodbye, angel.'

Baal pulled on the rope and Raphael's body was hauled by the neck, up into the reeking, smoke-filled air.

'Sleep well,' said Baal as he secured the rope and turned to go.

But Raphael was not done. As he died, the archangel summoned every ounce of his remaining power and threw it in Baal's face, hitting him with a dying curse so strong that the stone boiled beneath his feet.

'Is that it?' Baal had asked.

Raphael had smiled grimly at the archdemon through swollen lips before ceasing his struggles. The light disappeared from his eyes as Raphael Executor, the last archangel in Heaven, died.

'That was all too easy,' said Baal, humming to himself as he picked up Raphael's sword. 'Right, last one out turns off the lights.' He was almost at Heaven's gate before he realised what Raphael had done. The construct in which his soul resided was no longer a vessel to be occupied at a whim. Raphael's dying curse had locked him inside the shape of a boy angel with no way out. Baal was a captive inside a prison of his own making and he did not have the strength to break free.

The archdemon's scream of rage echoed around a ruined Heaven with no one left alive to hear it.

Jonathan's fingers slid away from Raphael's robe as he wept for all those who had been slaughtered by Baal's evil. One angel's despair had killed them all.

'Do you see now?' asked Darriel.

'I understand what happened, Dad,' said Jonathan, wiping his eyes and smearing ash across his face like a camouflage stripe. 'What I don't understand is what Baal wants with me.'

'He needs *power*, Jonathan, he needs your *wings*. While his soul is stuck in that perfect prison, his actual body is dying. The only thing that can save him is what locked him in there in the first place, and there's only one person left who can give him what he needs – *you*.'

Jonathan's face went white. 'He wants my wings? That maniac wants my wings! Let him try and take them, Dad. I fought Belial and I can fight Baal.'

'You could,' said Darriel. 'But even locked inside that construct Baal is incredibly dangerous. He always plans ahead and he's not taking any chances. He's unleashed the—'

Darriel stopped in mid-sentence as a deep vibration rang out across the ruins of Heaven; Jonathan felt it in both his head and his stomach. 'What was that?'

'It's Baal,' said Darriel. 'He's opened the gates of Heaven. We need to run back to Gabriel's workshop, Jonathan. We need to run *now*!'

The Hollow Angels

Jonathan, his father at his side, pelted along the boulevard towards the glass-shrouded building in the distance.

'Don't use your wings!' Darriel warned. 'It'll draw them to us like a magnet. They'll be on us in seconds.'

'Them?' asked Jonathan.

'It's what I was trying to tell you; powerful as he is Baal wouldn't take the risk of facing you alone. He's brought reinforcements with him.'

'Who?' asked Jonathan.

'He's reactivated the Cherubim,' said Darriel. 'My father's hollow angels are coming.'

Jonathan felt Gabriel's memories shudder inside his head. All he wanted was to flee this awful, death-filled place and get home with his father; to put as much distance as he could between them and yet another archdemon out for blood.

They were almost to the workshop when an awful screech tore across the ruins, shockingly loud after so much silence. Fear of what was following them now filled Jonathan, but also a strange desire to see his enemy face to face. It was so seductive that despite the danger, he almost stopped running so he could look over his shoulder.

'Don't listen to them!' his father ordered, grabbing Jonathan's arm and pulling him onward. He turned and stumbled towards the ruined garden, ash and bone crunching beneath his feet.

Another screech battered Jonathan's ears – this time much nearer. It was as if the Cherubim were calling to him, ordering him to surrender, to offer himself up. He clutched at his head in pain. Scrambling through the archway, he tripped over his own feet and fell face down in the cloying ash. As his father helped him up, he finally gave in to the urge to look behind him. There, far down the boulevard, was a blurry humanoid figure – its head sniffing the air like a dog.

Jonathan couldn't fully understand why, but the sight of the creature filled him with such revulsion that he almost vomited. It wasn't fear, or the ravaged landscape, but something else. The creature was simply . . . wrong. It was as though something beautiful had been taken and ruined, smeared with filth and given back to its owner, broken and twisted beyond all recognition.

'Please, son,' begged Darriel, dragging Jonathan into the workshop and pushing a heavy bench in front of the door.

'That's not going to stop them, Dad,' Jonathan panted.

'I know. We just need to slow them down as long as we can. Where's the gate to Hobbes End?'

'It's over in the far corner, inside a cupboard.'

'Then run for it!' shouted Darriel.

They sprinted across the workshop as fast as they could, slip-ping and sliding on the dusty floor as they hurtled along. They'd barely got halfway to safety when an enormous crash sounded from up above. A shower of glass and steel rained down as one of the Cherubim tore through the roof of Gabriel's workshop and slammed into the floor. Jonathan dived to one side to avoid being sliced in half by the sheets of falling glass while his father stumbled and fell beneath a nearby bench. Rolling to his feet, Jonathan stared in horror as he saw what stood between them and the way home.

It was over two metres tall, humanoid in shape, but smooth and oddly unfinished, like a shop mannequin. It wasn't what Jonathan was expecting though, not from the description that Sammael had given. He'd expected a being made from molten mercury, bright and shining like a sword, a walking weapon. The cherubim that stood in front of him was none of those things. Its skin was as mottled and leprous as a week-old corpse, and its wings hung slack against its back as if the effort of keeping them spread was too great to bear. But worst of all was the smell – it was worse than anything Jonathan had ever experienced, worse even than Belial. It stank of nothing more than corruption and death.

Jonathan stood frozen to the spot as the thing turned to look straight at him. He felt his throat shut tight in absolute horror as he found himself staring at a steel mask forged into the mockery of a human face, riveted to the cherubim's hairless skull. With an awful creaking sound, the mask grinned at him, then the thing took a step forward and spread its arms out wide.

That was when Darriel threw himself at it, driving it to its knees. 'Go, Jonathan!' he bellowed.

Knowing that to hesitate would be to die, Jonathan did as his father ordered and ran past. The cherubim shot out an arm and snagged Jonathan's ankle, sending him sprawling; its touch was cold and yet it burned like fire. He slammed hard against the floor, striking his head. With blood running from a cut above his eye he called to his wings, and they answered with a vengeance.

A writhing fan of imperial purple ribbons burst from his upper back, paused, then swatted the cherubim with extraordinary force. The creature flew skyward, tangling itself in the chains that dangled from the rafters while Jonathan's wing ribbons recoiled violently. He let out a grunt of pain; hitting that thing had hurt! What had Gabriel made it from?

'Let's go,' said Jonathan, grabbing his father's hand.

'Your wings . . .' gasped Darriel. 'I never believed they would be so—'

'Later, Dad!' shouted Jonathan.

They'd just begun to run when the thrashing creature above them raised its head and screeched again. This time, its call was answered. The wall ahead of them exploded inward and the two remaining Cherubim stalked into the workshop, their freakish, grinning masks scanning the room for prey.

'We're trapped,' Darriel gasped.

For a moment Jonathan almost despaired. He was so close to saving his dad, but something always seemed to get in the way.

It was then that he remembered where he was, and the weapons he had to hand. Acting on pure instinct, he plunged through a gap between two benches, reached out and slammed his hand against the pile of metal that lay curled up on the floor. There was no time for finesse, for gently singing sentience into being, piece by exquisitely crafted piece. Life was thrust violently into a sleeping titan and the dragon woke, screaming.

Jonathan ran back to his father as the skeletal construct reared up and bellowed. Only then did Jonathan realise that the dragon's roar was as much from pain as it was from rage. Mindless and in agony from such a violent birth, it ripped the chain-wrapped cherubim from where it hung before slamming it to the floor with a crash that shook the building. More glass showered down, and Jonathan and his father dived for cover.

'How did you do that?' Darriel gasped.

'I don't know,' said Jonathan, staring at the unfinished construct as it swung its awful head to face the other Cherubim. They launched themselves forward. Metal and wood flew in all directions as they attacked the dragon head-on. It reared and snapped at them with teeth the size of guillotine blades, but still they came – darting in to rip away small pieces of the dragon before it could retaliate.

The tail of the construct whipped round and sent flying the bench under which Jonathan and his father sheltered.

'Run, now!' shouted Darriel.

Not needing any further encouragement, Jonathan ran full-tilt towards the cupboard at the end of the aisle, his father at his side. They'd almost reached it when a terrible cry made them stop and look back. They saw a boy angel – his wings outstretched – hovering in the air above the raging dragon. In his right hand he held a long, slim sword whose blade rippled with a sickly green flame.

It was Baal, and the archdemon was staring at Jonathan with hungry eyes.

The dragon opened its jaws to bite the new arrival, but with a flick of his hand Baal sent a bolt of lurid energy flying from the end of his sword. It struck the construct full in the face, shattering the mighty head into red-hot fragments. Jonathan winced as the huge, metal skeleton dropped lifeless to the floor with a deafening crash.

Time slowed, and grabbing his father's hand, he sprinted for the cupboard. He knew that he couldn't fight Baal and the three Cherubim on his own. His only chance of getting out of Heaven in one piece was to make it through the gate.

'No escape!' shrieked Baal, and he launched a huge bolt of sizzling flame straight at the fleeing pair.

Jonathan wrenched open the door of the cupboard. He could see the gate to Hobbes End just ahead of him, could smell the village, hear someone's laughter. He turned to grab Darriel, but his eyes widened in horror as he saw a green fireball arc towards them.

Father and son just had time to look at each other before their world exploded with terrible fury. With a roar the entire workshop collapsed. It took some time for the dust to clear, but once it had, hanging in the air above the rubble were an arch-demon who looked like a young angel, and three monsters in steel masks.

'Find the boy and whoever that was who was helping him,' ordered Baal.

I Have a Secret

'How are you feeling, Sam?' asked Cay.

The angel looked at her and smiled. 'I feel like I've been run over by a bus. Smacking my head on a stone floor, and then the force of the gate slamming shut just as Jonathan yanked me to safety, was quite unpleasant.'

'He was really upset about losing his temper,' said Cay. 'He just wanted to find his dad so much. It's why he decided to go to Heaven on his own.'

'I know,' said Sammael, rubbing the bridge of her nose between thumb and forefinger. 'I wish he'd waited, though. After all these years, I have no idea what's on the other side of that back door he opened. I could have been a useful guide. Still, no point worrying about it now. Jonathan's obviously beginning to master his powers, as Mr Stubbs can attest. If he's not back by this evening then I'll climb up that ladder and go and look for him. I'm sure he'll be fine.'

Cay nodded, but there was something in Sammael's expression that said she had her doubts.

'The whole village knows what's happened, of course,' said

the angel. 'You can't keep something like this a secret. Still, at least Ignatius has warned everyone to keep their distance; better safe than sorry. Anyway, how did your first run with your father go?'

Cay gave her a shy smile. 'It was . . . I can't explain it really. It wasn't what I expected. I guess people think that werewolves just go around wanting to attack stuff, but it's not true. All I wanted to do was . . . run, and smell and hear things around me. It was so cool!'

'I'm sure it was,' grinned Sammael, turning to face Michael's window. They were sitting in the front pew of the church as the angel had wanted some peace and quiet until her head stopped hurting.

'There was another reason I asked to meet you here,' said Sammael.

'Oh?'

'Yes. I wanted to show you something, something that'll just be our secret. Can you keep a secret, Cay?'

'I think so,' she said, slightly unsure of whether she could or not. Some things were just so exciting that they couldn't remain secret for long.

Sammael raised her eyebrows. 'Are you sure?'

Cay nodded, her face serious. 'Yes, I'm sure.'

'Good,' said Sammael. 'I need to show you this. It's difficult to explain why I'm doing so but I'm worried. I have this awful feeling that something terrible is coming, something I haven't planned for, something I've missed.'

'Like what?'

'I don't know, Cay, but I have to do something to prepare, just in case. Remember what I said last night when I showed you the mirror in which my wings are imprisoned? About how it couldn't be broken?'

Cay nodded, her face alive with curiosity.

'The only way to break it is with a specific key that I made. Nothing else will suffice. It doesn't matter how powerful you are. The universe could end but that mirror would still be there, floating unharmed in nothingness.'

'And what is this key?' asked Cay.

'That's what I wanted to show you,' said Sammael, getting up from the pew and standing in front of the stained-glass window of Michael.

Cay watched in rapt attention as the angel held out her right hand and spoke.

'Little brother, I need the key you've kept for me since I left Hobbes End. It's time, Michael. I, Sammael Morningstar, ask it.'

Cay's eyes went wide in astonishment as Michael's image smiled at Sammael. He sank gracefully to one knee and spread out his wings before reaching back to pluck something from them. His stained-glass hand then reached *out* of the window – and he dropped a small, white object into the air. Sparkling in the sunlight, it gently spiralled down into Sammael's grasp.

'Thank you, little brother,' she whispered. She turned and walked back to Cay. 'Hold out your hand,' she said. Cay did as she was told, and Sammael held her lightly clenched fist above Cay's palm. 'How's this for a key?' she said, opening her fingers.

At first Cay didn't realise that there was something in her hand. Then she looked down, and there, nestling against her skin was a small, white feather, made from impossibly thin glass. 'It's an odd sort of key,' she said.

'It's tougher than it looks,' said Sammael. 'Who's going to think that you could break the impregnable with a feather made from glass?'

'Good point,' said Cay, grinning as she passed the feather back to Sammael.

The angel tucked it safely inside her coat. 'Right, I fancy a cup of tea. Let's pop over to the vicarage and see if—'

Suddenly, a terrible explosion rocked the church. A flash of sickly green light flared through Michael's window, casting awful shadows. Sammael looked at Cay, her face pale.

'What . . . ?' gasped Cay.

'It's Jonathan,' said Sammael. 'Something's happened to Jonathan!'

Ignatius and Grimm were walking across the green towards the shop when an incredible bang from the churchyard almost made them jump out of their skins.

'Dear God!' cried Ignatius.

'What the hell was that?' said Grimm, his ears ringing.

'I don't know,' said Ignatius. 'But it can't be good. Come on, let's go and find out.' He sprinted off at full speed, Grimm just behind him.

Racing into the churchyard they skidded to a halt, brought up short by a scene of devastation. The pile of rubble that had been Gabriel's cottage was now spread across a much greater area, and it was smoking as if subjected to great heat. The ladder was in pieces, and most terrible of all was the gate itself – it was *gone*.

A groan came from behind them and they turned to see Professor Morgenstern crumpled up against the flint wall of the church, blood running from a nasty gash on his forehead. Grimm kneeled next to him and whipped out a handkerchief to staunch the bleeding.

'Horatio, are you OK? Did you see what happened?' asked Ignatius.

The professor nodded. 'I was observing the gate and taking notes and then this big green flash came through and everything exploded! It wasn't me, was it?'

'No,' sighed Ignatius, his face distraught as he looked at the empty space in the air where the gate had hung. 'It wasn't your fault, Horatio. I think Jonathan must be in terrible trouble.'

'Oh dear,' sighed the professor, clutching his still-smouldering notebook to his chest. 'Oh dear, the poor boy.'

People flooded into the churchyard to see what had happened, Sammael and Cay at their head. 'Where's the gate gone?' cried Cay, utterly terrified. 'Where's Jonathan? He's not dead, is he?'

'I don't know,' said Sammael. 'I just don't know.'

'Listen to me,' said Grimm. 'Trying to stop Jonathan from looking for his dad would have been wrong. Something has happened and the gate has been shut, but don't forget who we're talking about here. He's a young lad, sure, but he's not helpless. He kicked Belial's scaly backside out of this world and into Hell itself and, personally, that's something I still find incredible. He's a fighter. I know it, and you know it.'

'What should we do, Grimm?' asked Cay.

'What we always do,' said the big man, gently cupping Cay's chin in his massive hand. 'We wait, we pray, and most importantly we make lots of tea. Whatever trouble Jonathan is in, he has the courage and the knowledge to get himself out of it.'

Cay nodded, but she couldn't help looking at where the gate had been and biting her lip.

'Is Elgar all right?' asked Professor Morgenstern.

'Elgar?' said Ignatius. 'He was here?'

The professor nodded. 'He was keeping me company. He kept trying to climb up the ladder and I had to keep lifting him off. He was just missing his friend, that's all; he didn't mean any harm.'

'Of course he didn't, Horatio, but where is he?'

Everyone started looking. The churchyard was a complete mess and there was plenty of debris that could conceal the body of a cat. A knocking sounded from over by the churchyard wall and the villagers turned to see Joanne Forrester striking a brick against a headstone. The look on her face was stricken as she signed to Cay.

'Oh God, no!' Cay cried as she ran to her mother, closely

followed by everyone else. She rounded the headstone, and there, lying still in the grass, was Elgar. His eyes were closed and a small trickle of blood ran from one ear. Half the fur had been singed from his tail and his breathing was horribly shallow.

Cay moved to pick the injured cat up but Grimm stopped her. 'Let me,' he said. 'He's still breathing and that's a good sign. I'll take him and the professor back to the vicarage, patch them up. It'll be OK, you'll see.'

Cay bit her lip to stop herself from crying as she watched Grimm gently pick up Elgar's limp form. Jonathan was trapped in Heaven and now Elgar and Professor Morgenstern had been hurt. This was not shaping up to be a good day at all.

'Kenneth, Joanne, would you please wait here and keep watch from a safe distance,' said Ignatius. 'Grimm, Sammael and I will be at the vicarage if anything happens.'

Cay's parents nodded.

'I'll wait too,' said Cay. Her mother smiled and wrapped an arm around her shoulders.

'It'll be all right, Cay,' Mr Forrester said reassuringly. 'Grimm was right about Jonathan. The lad's a fighter.'

Cay nodded, but she wondered if the time for Sammael to use that feather might be fast approaching.

The minutes passed slowly in the vicarage kitchen as Grimm tended to both Elgar and the professor. The gash on the professor's head was rapidly stitched up and he didn't appear to have concussion. Elgar was a different matter.

'I'm not a vet,' mumbled Grimm as he carefully examined the cat.

'You can say that again,' sighed Elgar, his eyes still closed. 'I'd have a better chance of survival if you ran me over with the car.'

'Oh, thank God!' gasped Grimm. 'I thought you were on your way out for a moment there.'

'Yeah, you wish,' grumbled the cat, slowly opening his eyes. He sniffed. 'What's that burning smell?'

'Um, it's probably your tail,' said Ignatius. 'It got a bit charred in the explosion. We've bandaged it up and hopefully the fur will grow back if you don't lick it constantly.'

Elgar got unsteadily to his feet and glanced at his damaged appendage. 'Could today actually get any worse?' he groaned. 'What happened, anyway? One minute I'm trying to sneak a peek into Heaven, and the next there's a big flash and I'm airborne.'

'The gate's been destroyed,' said Sammael, her face grave. 'Jonathan's trapped and I don't know how to help him.'

'And there we have today actually getting worse,' said the cat. 'Well, what do we do now?' He looked at Grimm, Ignatius and Sammael. Their faces told him all he needed to know. 'We just have to sit and wait again, don't we? I hate waiting so much!'

Trapped

Jonathan felt the awful weight of stone and steel against his wing ribbons. Without their incredible strength both he and his father would have been crushed to a pulp. He'd just had time to wrap them both head to toe before Baal's energy bolt had struck, blowing the cupboard and Gabriel's secret door to smithereens. The wing ribbons had taken the brunt of the blast, but Jonathan still felt as though he'd been hit by a truck. He wasn't concerned about his ability to dig his way out of the debris – his wings could deal with that – but what did worry him was the fact that Baal and the corrupted Cherubim might be waiting. Jonathan knew he was outmatched, especially with his father to protect.

He turned to look at Darriel. 'You OK, Dad?' he whispered. He seemed completely unharmed.

Darriel nodded and smiled. 'I did try to tell you how magnificent your wings were, earlier,' he said. 'I guess now's an even better time given that they're all that's standing between you and an unpleasant death. I'm glad I finally got to see them.' He paused and sighed. 'I'm sorry for everything your mum and I didn't tell you. We'd upset so many people by just being together that all we wanted to do was keep a low profile. We should have stayed with Gabriel like he asked us to.'

'It's OK, Dad,' said Jonathan. 'You didn't know what would happen.'

'I guess,' said Darriel. 'But we had plenty of warnings that Belial was coming for you. I suppose we were naïve in hoping that somehow we could just be normal, blend in with everyone else. We thought we were safe, and look what happened. Have you . . . have you heard from your mother at all?' Darriel's face suddenly wore a haunted look.

Jonathan had to fight hard not to let his eyes well up. 'No,' he croaked. 'All I know is that she went to Hell to try and ask Lucifer for help. Then she just disappeared. Not even Lucifer knows where she is.'

'You met Lucifer?' Darriel gasped.

'He visited Hobbes End yesterday to attend Gabriel's memorial service and get a look at me, see what all the fuss was about. He wound me up so much I broke his nose.'

Darriel's eyes looked like they might pop out of his head. 'I assume the fact that you're still in one piece means Lucifer didn't get angry with you?'

'He just wanted to see whether I'd stick up for myself,' said Jonathan. 'He finds me interesting apparently.'

Darriel gave his son a sad smile. 'Savantha and I really did create someone amazing in you,' he said. 'We couldn't be more proud. Promise me you'll try to find her once you get out of here.'

'Of course I will, Dad. We can do it together though, can't we? You're not too hurt, are you?'

Darriel just stared back at Jonathan, his mouth half open as if he wanted to say something but couldn't.

'I saw the blood and the drag marks outside Heaven's gates, Dad. Who helped you, and why did you say that you're stuck here? What are you not telling me?'

'I—' Jonathan's father began, but a grinding of metal on stone interrupted him. 'Baal's not giving up,' said Darriel, his face grim. 'He'll have the Cherubim sorting through the rubble to see if you made it through the gate to Hobbes End. He'll see your wings, son, and then he'll tear them from you.'

Jonathan knew that his father was right. If he hid his wings there was less likelihood they'd be seen, but if he did that they'd be instantly squashed. He felt a sudden shift in pressure as some debris was removed from above them.

'If we can't move then we'll just have to hide,' said Jonathan.

'How do we do that?' asked Darriel.

'I need to talk to Gabriel; I'll be back in a second.'

'You need to do what?' asked Darriel.

But Jonathan wasn't listening. In his mind he was already sitting in a library chair and focusing on a single word, *camouflage*. This time he didn't even have to hunt for the book. His will was focused, and he knew exactly what he needed:

A treatise on quantum light refraction
Or, Hiding in plain sight, by G Artificer.

'Gotcha,' he said under his breath.

'Jonathan, what are you doing?' asked Darriel.

'I'm making sure that those Cherubim don't see us. They'll think we're just another lump of rock.'

'How is that possible?'

'These wings and Grandfather's knowledge,' said Jonathan. 'He transferred everything he knew to me when he died.'

'So he finally managed to figure it out,' said Darriel, his voice touched with awe. 'I knew that he wanted to leave it all to you, but I didn't know that he'd perfected the method.' He took a deep breath. 'I'm sorry you didn't get the chance to know him properly. Your mother and I should just have done what he suggested and come to Hobbes End to be with him. Our stubbornness cost you so much.'

'I would have liked to have known Gabriel better, Dad,' said Jonathan. 'But he'll always be with me. It wasn't your fault everything happened the way it did – that was all down to Belial. And he's been dealt with.'

'What happened to him?' asked Darriel.

'I dropped him on Lucifer's tower, and then Lucifer turned Belial's head into a wall-mounted trophy. We got our payback, Dad!'

Darriel opened his mouth to reply when there was a loud clang from just above them. 'Here they come,' said Jonathan. 'Keep quiet and still while I hide us.' He closed his eyes, and let the formulae from the latest book flow from his mind and out through his wing ribbons. The purple glow faded to be replaced by the dusty-grey striations of dressed stone. Not only that, but the wings exuded a field that dulled a viewer's senses, made them ignore what was under their nose. *Don't see me*, they whispered into the ether. 'Here's hoping this works on constructs and arch-demons,' Jonathan whispered to his father.

The crashing sounds of metal, glass and stone being lifted and thrown aside grew steadily louder, and Jonathan felt the pressure on his wings fade away.

'They're almost here,' he said.

Wrapped in their cocoon, Jonathan and his father held their breath as the Cherubim, worked into a frenzy by Baal's orders, dug at incredible speed.

'Clear it, damn you!' Baal shouted. 'Find me the bodies of the boy and whoever was stupid enough to be helping him. They must be down there somewhere and I need to feed!'

Jonathan shuddered and stifled a yelp as he felt the cocoon of his wings grabbed roughly, lifted as though it weighed nothing at all and thrown into the air. There was a moment of weight-lessness before they crashed into the remains of the workshop with jarring force. Despite the protection provided by his camou-flaged wings, Jonathan had to stifle a cry of pain from the impact. Seconds later, an inhuman shriek tore through the silence.

'What do you mean, you can't find them?' shouted Baal.

There was no reply from the Cherubim that Jonathan could hear.

'But he must be here. *HE MUST BE!*' screamed the arch-demon. Random bolts of green fire flew in all directions. 'No, no, no!' roared Baal. 'He can't have escaped back to Hobbes End. I almost had him. And that man who was with him, he looked just like . . . no, no that's impossible. I turned this place into a mausoleum!'

Jonathan listened to the archdemon as he ranted and raved. Baal's voice wasn't just filled with insane fury; there was something else in there too – desperation.

'Well, I know where he is now,' said Baal. 'I didn't want to do it this way, but so be it. Once I've finished there'll be nothing left of Hobbes End but a smoking crater in the middle of a charred forest. This construct body hid my true nature from Heaven and it'll do the same with the village. You three, come with me. We have work to do.'

Jonathan's heart leaped into his mouth. Oh God, no! he thought. He's going to attack the village and I'm not even there.

There was a last clatter of shifting debris and then silence.

'Do you think he's gone?' asked Darriel.

'I'll have a look,' said Jonathan, opening a tiny crack in his wings so he could peep out. All he could see was the shattered remains of his grandfather's workshop. The sight made him feel desperately sad. 'Looks like the coast is clear, Dad,' he said. 'C'mon, we need to get out of here.'

'The only chance we have are Heaven's main gates,' said Darriel. 'Maybe Baal won't have locked them behind him, given that he's fixated on trying to find you.'

Jonathan nodded. 'Let's go and see,' he said, his wings blinking out of existence.

They clambered down from the pile of rubble on which they'd landed and made their way back towards the side door. There was no easy route given the destruction that had been visited on the building, but eventually Jonathan and his father emerged into the ruined garden.

'We need to get moving, Dad. I've got to warn everyone back at the village that Baal is coming. They won't have time to prepare a defence. He could be there already!'

'I know, son,' said Darriel. 'Let's go.'

They ran back down the stricken boulevard, avoiding the bones of the dead as best they could. The horror of it all hadn't faded, but Jonathan knew there was nothing he could do for Heaven right now. The damage had already been done and he had a duty to the living.

They reached the great tree and Jonathan stopped near to the hanging body of Raphael. 'It's not right to just leave him there,' he said to his father.

'No,' said Darriel. 'You're right. No matter what Raphael did, this is . . . cruelty for cruelty's sake.'

Jonathan summoned his wings and carefully cradled Raphael's body while he used a wing ribbon to slice through the rope that held him aloft. Lowering the dead angel to the ground, he gently laid him at the base of the tree, his arms across his chest. 'I'm sorry for what you suffered, Raphael,' he said softly. 'I'll tell Sammael what happened to you.'

'Come on,' said Darriel. 'We need to hurry.'

Nodding his agreement, Jonathan got to his feet and followed his father along an even wider boulevard. It didn't take Jonathan long to recognise it. 'I was here in my dream,' he said.

'It's where the carnage started,' said Darriel. 'Baal is evil in body and soul. This is a game to him.'

'He's an archdemon, so it's in his nature,' sighed Jonathan.

Darriel looked at him quizzically.

'It's what Belial said to me when I asked him why he had caused so much pain,' said Jonathan.

'I'm glad you made him pay for what he did,' said Darriel. 'I am proud of you, my son.'

Jonathan smiled at his father. 'We'll have time to talk about it once we get back home and stop Baal,' he said as he jogged onwards.

Darriel looked at his son's back and blinked his eyes, unable to cry even if he wanted to. 'Time is the one thing we don't have, my amazing boy,' he whispered.

They continued on, and after rounding a corner Jonathan was hugely relieved to see the gates of Heaven appear before him out of the smoke-filled gloom. They towered upwards, piercing the clouds and disappearing from view.

'Finally!' he said, running until he could place his hands on the extraordinary glass. The quantum equations were still in there, flowing forever downward. In the centre of the gates, level with Jonathan's head, was a pair of carved-glass handles. He grabbed them and pulled as hard as he could but the gates wouldn't budge.

'Baal's locked them, Dad!' cried Jonathan.

'I was afraid of that,' said Darriel. 'Baal is using Raphael's sword to command the gates to stay shut.'

'Then how do we get out?'

'I don't know,' said Darriel.

Jonathan kept his hands gripped on the handles. 'There's got to be a way,' he said. 'My grandfather was Gabriel Artificer, and he'd know if I could open these gates without Raphael's sword.' He was about to go back into the library inside his head when he realised he didn't need to. He could feel the construction of the gates beneath his hands, sense the stream of celestial mechanics contained within them. Somehow, it all seemed incredibly familiar.

'Who built these gates?' he asked his father.

'Lucifer did,' said Darriel. 'He was the first of us. These gates were his glory.'

'But the way they're put together,' said Jonathan. 'It feels like something Gabriel would have come up with.' He sank his mind into the warp and weft of the gates, speaking directly to the flow of information that formed their heart. 'I am of Gabriel's blood. You might not believe me but you've been tricked. The monster that holds Raphael's sword is no angel; he has destroyed Heaven.'

The gates shuddered under his hands; they were listening to him.

'I'm sorry for striking you earlier when I was outside. I was worried about my dad but I've found him now. I need to go home and save my friends from Baal. He's the one responsible for all this. The body of Raphael Executor is lying on the ground under that huge tree; he showed me what happened here. You know I'm telling the truth.'

There was the longest pause before the gates replied. And then they howled in anguish. They were like Hobbes End, but not as sentient. They just did as they were told, but they cared about what they guarded. Through Jonathan, they could see that they had failed, that Heaven had been devastated and every angel slaughtered. Shaking with fury and effort, they ignored the orders they had been designed to obey, even though they knew the price would be high.

Cracks began to appear in the glass. They grew in size and speed until it sounded like an explosion in a window factory. The gates wanted to let Jonathan out; they recognised him as a maker, a builder, an engineer – just like the one who had created them back at the beginning of time. Rules were rules, but sometimes rules were meant to be broken.

The incredible glass of Heaven's gate sang in pain before exploding outward into a void filled with stars. Shards full of quantum mathematics skittered across the polished marble only to fade and die right in front of Jonathan's eyes. If it hadn't been so important that he get to Hobbes End, he would have wept at what he'd had to do. The way out was in front of him, and he turned to take his father's hand.

Darriel shook his head as around and behind him myriad spheres of blue light blossomed into life.

'Dad?' said Jonathan, his voice breaking.

Darriel looked at his son in a way that only a father could, with love, pride and regret for the mistakes he'd made. 'Deep down you knew, Jonathan; you just didn't want to believe it.'

Jonathan bowed his head. His father was telling the truth and it hurt so much he wanted to curl up into a ball and cry. He looked at Darriel; behind him, where there should have been footprints in the ash, there was nothing. His father had been mortally injured by Belial, and yet here he was, apparently fine. Finally Baal's comment about recognising Darriel but not knowing how this could be finally made sense.

'I was too late, wasn't I?' Jonathan sobbed, finally giving in.

Darriel walked over and put his arms round his son. 'I was gone before you had a chance to do anything about it,' he said. 'Baal dragged me inside this ruin and watched me die.'

Jonathan let out an awful cry, holding onto his father with all his strength. 'It's not fair,' he sobbed. 'I was supposed to rescue you, Dad.'

'I know, my boy, but there was nothing you could have done. The restless dead here in Heaven gave my soul form so I could help you. They've been trapped in this prison for such a long time, but in opening the gates – something I could not do – you have freed them. Now it is their turn to help you.'

'What do you mean?' cried Jonathan.

'Your home is under threat. If you do not leave now it may be too late. Go and save Hobbes End, my incredible boy. Take the wrath of Heaven with you. Defeat Baal and save your mother. I know she is not dead, for I would have felt it. Do it for me, my son.'

The ground began to shake as the blue spheres around Darriel coalesced into a vast cloud. 'Don't be afraid,' he said. 'Let the dead have their vengeance and I can finally rest. Now I have seen you again I have no rage left, only love for you and your mother.'

Too bereft to know what to say, Jonathan stood between the shattered gates of Heaven and watched the approaching cloud. He could see faces in it: men, women, children, all crying out to be free.

'Goodbye, Jonathan,' said Darriel. 'I will be with you, always.'

'Dad!' cried Jonathan. 'I don't want to—'

And then the cloud struck him, lifted him off his feet and over the edge of the marble steps. The universe spread out before him and he fell headlong into it.

Darriel stood and watched as the cloud carried his son away. 'Goodbye, my boy,' he whispered to the stars. There was a crunch of glass as a figure with huge, bat-like wings sprouting from his shoulders dropped softly to the plaza. Lucifer stepped forward, his face impassive but his eyes burning like the sun. He stood amidst the shards of the gates he had built and stared at the remains of Heaven, and at the distant body of Raphael lying on a bed of ash.

'How did this happen?' he asked.

'Baal,' replied Darriel. 'He made Raphael despair and this is the result. You could have prevented it, had your pride not blinded you to what was happening under your nose.'

Lucifer clenched his fists and his face darkened. For a moment he looked as though he might explode, but instead he sighed and bowed his head. 'Baal will pay for this atrocity,' he whispered.

'I hope so,' said Darriel. 'It would make me happy to know that you might finally stop sulking and help my son. Are you going to sit and watch as Sammael and Jonathan – a wingless archangel and a young boy – face an archdemon and the corrupted Cherubim?'

'I . . . I . . .' Lucifer stammered.

'That's the trouble with pride,' said Darriel, his body fading as his soul began its long journey back to the heart of creation. 'It always comes before a fall. And you, the first Morningstar, have fallen so very, very far. Maybe it's time you started to climb back up into the light? See if you can help save the creation you brought into being?'

Lucifer said nothing, but the conflict on his face was obvious.

'Goodbye,' said Darriel, and then he was gone, leaving Lucifer to stand alone, surrounded by the wreckage of all he had once loved.

The Gathering Storm

S ammael was sitting on a bench in her garden when the sails of the windmill gave an ominous creak. The angel looked up, her hair whipped about by a fitful gust of wind. She had ordered the sails to stay still, but something more than wind was tugging at them, making them uneasy.

Sammael got to her feet, opened the garden gate and strode across the green. As she passed the pond she noticed that the waters were choppy and restless. 'What's up, Hobbes End?' she said. 'What do you know that I don't?' She headed for the vicarage and wasn't at all surprised to see Ignatius, Grimm and Elgar walking down the drive to meet her. 'Something's wrong,' she said to them. 'I can't put my finger on it but it feels like the village is afraid.'

'I agree,' said Ignatius. 'And this wind' – he raised a hand into the blustery air and brought his fingertips to his nose – 'smells greasy and burned.'

'Like . . . ashes,' said Sammael, her face going white.

'This is something to do with Jonathan, isn't it?' said Grimm.

'It's too much of a coincidence for it not to be,' said Sammael.

She looked up at the sky. 'Do those clouds look right to you?' she asked, watching as a darkening swirl began to form directly over the village.

'No, they don't,' said Ignatius. 'What on earth is causing it?'

'Nothing on Earth,' said Sammael. 'I think something from Heaven is coming to pay us a visit.'

'Is it Jonathan?' asked Elgar.

'No,' said the angel. 'I don't know what this is. I've never felt anything like it before.' She shut her eyes and concentrated as the wind began to shriek around her. When she opened them again, she looked very afraid. 'No, I'm mistaken. I *have* felt something like it before, at Armageddon. It's malice incarnate and it's getting closer.'

'What do you mean?' asked Ignatius.

'There's only one thing that exudes such a terrible aura, and that's an archdemon.'

'*What?*' barked Ignatius. 'How is that possible? Why is it coming from the direction of Heaven? And what's happened to Jonathan? Is he all right?'

Sammael shook her head. 'I don't have the answers,' she said. 'But we have little time to prepare. As for Jonathan, all I know is that he must be OK. He's linked to the village very deeply now, and Hobbes End would know if he was . . . had been badly hurt.'

'Well, that's something,' said Grimm. 'What do we do now?'

'Get everyone into the church,' said Sammael. 'It's stronger than it looks – Gabriel helped rebuild it after his arrival and he made some improvements – and it'll be safer than anywhere else. Montgomery, Stubbs, station yourselves on the roof of the lych gate. Make sure everyone gets in safely.'

'Yes, ma'am,' said Stubbs, obeying his orders without question.

'See, told you he'd come round on the whole sir–ma'am, thing,' grinned Montgomery, before leaping off after his friend.

'And, gentlemen?'

'Yes,' said the two men in unison.

'Bring me your rapier and cricket bat; I think we may need some help with what's coming!'

'Everyone inside. Hurry!' shouted Ignatius. He stood by the lych gate, and with the gargoyles' help shepherded the inhabitants of Hobbes End into the church. Over his shoulder he cast anxious glances at the thunderous sky.

'Are you sure it's a good idea to have everyone in the same place?' asked Grimm, finishing a sweep of the village to make sure that nobody had been left behind.

'If Sam says it's the safest place then it makes sense to me,' said Ignatius.

'Hmm,' said Grimm. 'I hope you're right.' He looked up at the sky. 'Those clouds are all wrong. They're moving the opposite way to the wind!'

They all jumped as a bolt of lightning flashed from the growing maelstrom above to strike the lightning rod on top of the windmill. A terrific crack of thunder shook the village.

'Whatever's coming is almost here!' shouted Sammael, running over to them. 'But we are not defenceless.' She returned Ignatius's rapier and Grimm's cricket bat to the two men. 'I hope you don't mind, but I dipped them in the pond and asked the village to beef them up for you. You'll find that the sword has a particularly keen edge now, and that the cricket bat has a distinct punch. The effects won't last long, but they should be effective in an emergency.'

Ignatius and Grimm grinned at each other.

'Right, I need to go,' said Sammael.

'Be careful, Sam,' said Cay, as she ran over from the church and gave the angel a hug. 'Are you going to use the feather?' she whispered in Sammael's ear.

'I think I may have to, Cay. Now, stay with your parents and keep under cover. Don't you dare get yourself hurt.'

'I promise,' said Cay.

'What should I do?' asked Elgar.

'Try not to get struck by lightning!' chuckled Grimm. 'Your tail's already a mess.'

To emphasise the point, another incandescent flash reduced a tree on the far side of the green to a smouldering pile of wood chips. Elgar yowled and threw himself behind Grimm's legs.

'I've got to go,' said Sammael. 'Don't do anything stupid, will you?'

'Us?' said Grimm.

'And what are you going to do, Sam?' asked Ignatius.

'I'm going to do something dear Gabriel wouldn't have had the strength to accomplish. It will take an enormous amount of effort on my part, and I won't be able to maintain it for long, but it will give Jonathan time to get back to us before it's too late.' Giving them all a gentle smile, she ran back across the green towards the pond.

'Right then,' said Grimm. 'We've got new, improved toys.' He brandished Isobel for emphasis. 'I wonder what I can do with this now?'

'I think we're about to find out!' shouted Ignatius. The wind suddenly increased in force. Trees bent sideways, leaves and dust billowed through the air and a dozen lightning bolts struck all over the village, one of them shattering the chimney pot on Mr and Mrs Flynn's cottage. The storm reached a howling crescendo and then, suddenly, fell utterly silent.

High in the sky above the village green, a nightmare burst into view. Ignatius and Grimm could only stare in disbelief as what looked like a child angel and three grotesque humanoid creatures tore through the boiling clouds at incredible speed. The angel, his face a mask of insane hatred, screamed incoherently as he plunged downward. In his hand, a delicate glass sword that could have been the twin of Ignatius's rapier glowed a lurid green.

'What the hell are they?' gasped Grimm.

'*Oh no!*' cried Montgomery.

'What's the matter?' asked Elgar.

'They're screaming inside. They hate themselves; they hate what they have been turned into but they can't stop. Our brothers have become monsters!'

'Your brothers?' hissed Elgar.

'Yes,' said Stubbs, the expression on his face one of utter horror. 'Gabriel's perfect constructs. *It's the Cherubim!*'

'And that child,' said Ignatius. 'Didn't Jonathan say there was a boy angel in his nightmare?'

'Yes,' said Grimm. 'He did. And now it looks like whatever Jonathan met in Heaven has decided to pay us a visit. Everyone inside the church; we are in serious trouble!'

'ABOMINATION!' Sammael screamed as she saw what had appeared in the sky. She didn't know what appalled her most: the twisted mockery of the Cherubim, or the boy angel who wielded Raphael's sword of authority, radiating menace like a black sun. She had felt that evil before, stared in its face across a vast battlefield. She could never forget the despair that had flowed from the archdemon. 'Baal!' she spat.

Dropping to her knees by the edge of the pond, Sammael drove her hands into the ground, seeking the power that lay there. Joining her will to that of the village, she did something quite extraordinary. From around the outskirts of Hobbes End, a curtain of shimmering, white force sprang upward in a huge hemisphere. Inside it, the flow of mathematical symbols wrote themselves across the bruised sky.

Baal saw what was happening and increased his downward plunge along with the Cherubim, his rage so strong that everyone in the village could feel it. It was vast and incoherent, blind and utterly savage.

The edges of the curtain raced to meet themselves at a point high above the kneeling Sammael. Her eyes narrowed as she funnelled every ounce of her concentration into protecting the village. She looked up and saw the edges about to meld, but her sigh of relief turned to a gasp of horror as the Cherubim suddenly increased speed. With only centimetres to spare, two of them managed to plunge through the tiny gap before it slammed shut.

With a crash that rattled every window in the village, Baal struck the shield. An explosion of green fire lanced across the sky and Sammael groaned with the effort of holding the shimmering dome intact. Baal screamed and screamed, battering the shield with his sword in total frenzy. For a moment, the flow of quantum formulae arching overhead buckled and tore under the onslaught, but the shield held.

Sammael allowed herself a weak smile, a smile that lasted until one of the Cherubim slammed to the ground scant metres away. She got to her feet and turned to confront the living weapon that wore a grinning steel mockery of a face. 'You're mine,' she said.

'Incoming!' yowled Elgar as the second cherubim streaked across the village towards them.

Grimm adjusted the angle of his bowler hat, took a wide-legged stance and raised Isobel over his right shoulder. 'Okey-dokey,' he said. 'Let's hope the *adjustments* Sammael made are sufficient!'

'If I didn't know better,' said Ignatius, holding his rapier at the ready, 'I'd swear you were enjoying this.'

Grimm flashed Ignatius a wicked grin, before letting out an ear-splitting battle cry and running straight at the enemy.

'Oh God, here we go again,' said Elgar.

And for the second time in as many weeks, Hobbes End began the fight of its life.

The Battle of Hobbes End:
Part Two

The cherubim that had landed by the pond strode towards Sammael, the mask that covered its face smiling horribly. Without waiting for the construct to reach her, Sammael leaped forward, rammed her fingers into the eyeholes of its mask and tore it from the cherubim's face. It shrieked in pain, clapping its hands to the livid skin beneath – it was as if the sunlight that had once helped create the cherubim now burned it to the core. Its dead, black eyes fixed themselves on the furious angel as she held up the steel mask. In a gesture of total contempt she dropped it to the grass and crushed it beneath her boot.

'You have been corrupted,' she said. 'My brother and I did not create you to be an archdemon's lackey!'

It tilted its head to one side as if listening, then threw itself forward and dealt Sammael a blow that knocked her into the air.

She crashed to the ground some metres away, ploughing a wide furrow across the green as she came to a stop. She clambered painfully to her feet, the cherubim watching her dispassionately.

Wiping a trickle of blood from her bottom lip, Sammael nodded to herself.

'So it's going to be like that, is it?' she asked. The cherubim didn't respond. 'Fair enough,' she said, before delivering a lightning-fast kick direct to the construct's midriff. It folded up and flew backwards, landing in a crumpled heap by the edge of the pond.

With odd, disjointed movements, the cherubim stood upright and looked at its chest. A patch of its rotting, metallic flesh had been torn away, and droplets of what looked like liquid mercury seeped from the wound.

Sammael favoured the cherubim with a grim smile. 'You're in my home now, construct,' she said. 'Shielded from him.' She pointed upward to the gibbering Baal as he lashed out impotently at the shield. 'Welcome to Hobbes End, and the day of your unmaking!'

The cherubim nodded its understanding, its inhuman eyes and raw, unformed features turning the simple gesture into something repulsive. Sammael braced herself for the inevitable attack, but instead felt a profound disgust as the cherubim dug a hand into the wound on its chest. It withdrew its fingers – now dripping with silvery gore – and held them up to its face as if for inspection.

'What the—?' said Sammael, not understanding the creature's actions.

With extraordinary speed, the construct flicked its hand straight at Sammael's face, sending metallic droplets flying into her eyes.

The archangel clapped her hands to her face and screamed as the cherubim's corrupt blood burned its way into her flesh, flooding her mind with scenes of madness . . .

Cay stood next to her father as he changed into his wolf form, and watched as the second cherubim flew straight towards Grimm. At the last moment, the big man ducked and swung Isobel with all his might. With a sound like an anvil being struck with a blacksmith's hammer, the bat hit the cherubim across its back and knocked it flying into the church tower. Flint and mortar rained down as the stunned creature fell to land in a heap on the grass.

'Blimey!' said Elgar. 'Sam wasn't wrong about beefing up the weaponry!'

Grimm held the bat up and kissed its scarred surface. 'There's my girl,' he said proudly.

'Don't get carried away,' said Ignatius. 'That was too easy.'

Grimm nodded, but his excitement about the potential for damage he could inflict with the upgraded Isobel was obvious. He ran forward to make sure that the cherubim stayed down, but just as he reached it, it opened its eyes and launched itself into the air. Grimm just had time to register disbelief before the construct knocked him flying. Tumbling through the air, he was brought to an abrupt halt by a large headstone; he struck it with a sickening crunch, fell to the ground and lay groaning.

'*Grimm!*' cried Ignatius, launching himself at the battered cherubim. It turned to face him, its grotesque mask dented and knocked askew by the impact with the church. Ignatius didn't pause; once again he was up against an enemy who could slay him on the spot, and yet he swallowed his fear – he had a church full of villagers to protect and he could not afford weakness.

He'd barely taken two steps when Montgomery and Stubbs streaked ahead of him to intercept the construct. Stubbs rugby-tackled the creature at speed, knocking it off its feet and pinning it to the ground.

Montgomery leaped onto the cherubim's chest and grabbed hold of its head, but instead of hitting it he cried out in anguish, 'Brother, please stop! You've forgotten what you are. We have the same creator; we don't want to hurt you! Please . . .'

Cay could hear the pain in the little gargoyle's voice. If Montgomery had tear ducts he would have been weeping.

Ignatius stood still and watched in amazement as the cherubim froze. It was listening to the gargoyle.

'Brother, Gabriel wouldn't want this. You don't have to obey that thing up there.' Montgomery pointed to Baal where he hung in the sky above the shield. '*That* is not your maker. He has hurt you, changed you, but you don't have to obey him. Remember what you are!'

The cherubim raised its arm and gently touched the little gargoyle's face. Its steel mask ceased its awful grinning, and changed to an expression of utter torment.

'Come with me and Mr Stubbs,' Montgomery begged.

For a second it looked as though the creature might do as it was asked, but a howl of fury from Baal shattered whatever small measure of peace it might have found. Its mask turned into a twisted, snarling face as it swatted Montgomery away like a fly. The gargoyle crashed through one of the side windows of the church, bounced off an oak beam and fell to the floor with a huge crash, shattering the flagstones beneath him.

Stubbs just had time to look surprised before the cherubim surged upright and kicked him across the churchyard like a football. The gargoyle ricocheted off the wall and ploughed through the roof of the lych gate, before landing in a crumpled heap on the road. He sat up, and his previously undamaged ear fell off his head and into his lap. '*Oh, come on! Really?*' he shouted before getting unsteadily to his feet . . .

Kenneth Forrester blocked the doorway of the church with his massive wolf body, making sure that the cherubim couldn't get past. Over his shoulder, his wife, Elgar and the rest of the villagers peered anxiously at the carnage that had visited their home.

Ignatius advanced once again, but a terrible scream came from the direction of the pond.

'Sam!' cried Cay. Without a moment's thought, she reached for the wolf inside her and called it forth. Her clothes were shredded as she changed shape and dashed past her father, a red-furred blur as she shot through the ruined lych gate.

Kenneth howled at her and made to follow, but didn't want to leave the church vulnerable. He snarled, and ground his fangs in indecision as to who he needed to protect most. He was spared further torment when Montgomery ran underneath him to re-join Stubbs who had just staggered back into the churchyard.

'Go help Cay and Sam!' Ignatius shouted over his shoulder. With a growl of assent, Mr Forrester tore after his daughter.

Ignatius returned his attention to the cherubim as it strode towards him. It was difficult to imagine that this rotting thing had been one of Gabriel's triumphs, however bittersweet, but Ignatius was glad that the construct was a shadow of its former self. If it had been at full strength, then it would have killed them all in seconds.

'What do we do, guv?' asked a very annoyed Stubbs.

'Watch my back,' said Ignatius. 'I want to try something.' Realising that brute force wasn't going to work, the vicar decided to use finesse. Before the construct could get any closer he ducked and rolled to one side before lashing out with his rapier. He expected to feel resistance, shock even, just as he had when he'd fought Raven – one of the Corvidae – but this wasn't the case. With an edge now so sharp it could slice a mote of dust in two, his rapier bit into the cherubim's side and sliced it open like a ripe cheese. Sickly grey fluid burst from the wound, and the creature stopped to look at the damage. It was as if it was surprised that it could be hurt.

The cherubim turned back to face Ignatius, and the expression on its mask changed to one of complete and utter savagery. With arms outstretched, it launched itself forward to pound Ignatius into a pulp. It had almost closed the gap when Isobel connected with the side of its head, knocking it sideways with an awful crunch. The construct folded up like a rag doll before once more making solid contact with the wall of the church.

'I hope that hurt!' spat Grimm, furious from being slammed into a headstone. 'Look what you've done to my hat.' He held out the bowler he'd taken from Rook of the Corvidae, showing the cherubim the damage it had caused. The brim was dented and torn and a large hole was punched into the crown. 'That was my favourite.'

'Has it occurred to you,' shouted Elgar, 'that the hat just saved you from a fractured skull?'

'Humph,' snorted Grimm, not mollified in the slightest.

'Oh God!' said Ignatius as the cherubim started to rise once again.

'What?' asked Grimm.

'It wants to die,' said Ignatius. 'It can't disobey Baal's orders but it knows that what it's doing is wrong.'

'How do you know that?' asked Grimm.

'The village can tell,' said Ignatius, looking at the grey fluid spattered across the ancient stonework of the church. 'It can read it in the construct's blood. The cherubim hates what it's been turned into but can't stop itself. It wants us to do it.'

'That's right,' said Montgomery, his voice quiet and sad. 'It wants to be unmade. Oh, brother . . .' Stubbs put a reassuring paw on his friend's shoulder.

'How do we unmake this thing before it kills us?' said Grimm as the cherubim got to its feet.

'I don't know,' said Ignatius, casting a glance at the shield high above, where it rang and buckled under Baal's relentless onslaught. 'I just don't know.'

The construct flew at them once more, diving low and knocking them both off their feet. Ignatius swung his rapier but the cherubim grabbed the blade with its left hand. The steel bit deep, severing two fingers, but it gave the construct enough leverage to twist the sword violently from Ignatius's grasp. The vicar gave a cry as the bones in his wrist came within a whisker of breaking, and watched as his rapier was flung out over the churchyard. With its other hand, the cherubim grasped Grimm around the throat, forcing him to the ground. Grimm thrashed this way and that, trying to break the construct's grip, but it was like arguing with an oak tree. The gargoyles leaped in to help, tugging at the cherubim's hand away, but it was too strong. Grimm's face went purple, and Ignatius staggered to his feet just in time to see a black blur streak from the church porch.

'Elgar, *no!*' bellowed the vicar.

The cat ignored him. With glorious abandon, he grabbed hold of the cherubim with all claws, and sank his teeth deep into the wound in its side. Before the construct could react, Elgar braced his back feet against its chest and launched himself away, something gripped between his teeth. Behind him, a long, thin ribbon unravelled from inside the wound. The cherubim made a half-hearted grasp with its maimed hand but failed to get a grip on the slippery material.

It ceased trying to strangle Grimm and watched as Elgar raced away, the expression on its mask changing to one of peace. The ribbon got longer and longer until the end pulled free from the cherubim's body with an audible snap. With a sigh, it dropped to the ground like a sack of potatoes – utterly lifeless.

'Ptooey!' spat Elgar. 'That tastes like I've been licking road kill. Don't touch that, by the way,' he called out, nodding at the mercury-streaked ribbon that trailed across the churchyard. 'I'm a demon, and that silvery gunk even makes me feel a bit weird, I don't think you'd like it.'

Everyone looked at Elgar in stunned silence.

'What?' asked the cat.

Climbing to his feet, Grimm put the wrecked bowler hat on his head and rubbed his throat. 'What did you just *do*?' he asked, amazed at his sudden reprieve.

'I used my brain,' said Elgar, grinning widely. 'It may have been rotting away, but that thing is still a killing machine. I saw something sticking out of that wound on its side and thought I recognised it. I figured that if I gave it a good yank then it may give us a helping hand. I wasn't expecting such a dramatic result, though.'

Ignatius tottered over to where the ribbon lay on the grass. He looked at it with astonishment. Beneath the coating of the cherubim's blood the ribbon was strangely familiar. There, barely visible beneath the stained surface, flowed a series of mathematical symbols. Ignatius looked up to the shield overhead; the same symbols flowed there too.

'Of course,' he said. 'I'd forgotten how Gabriel powered these monstrosities.'

'Yeah,' said Elgar. 'He cut off three of his wing ribbons and put one into each of the constructs. I bet that hurt!'

Ignatius nodded his agreement when a terrible howl came from the village green. 'Oh no!' he shouted. 'Sam, Cay and Kenneth are fighting the other one; we need to go help them, now!'

Cay flew across the green, the wind rippling her fur as she saw the cherubim standing over the prone Sammael. The angel was clawing at her eyes and moaning in pain, oblivious to the fact that she was about to die. The cherubim had just raised its foot to stamp the life out of Sammael when Cay jumped onto its back and sank her teeth into its shoulder, thrashing her head to inflict as much damage as possible.

Surprised and knocked off balance, the cherubim fell to the grass next to the wounded angel. Cay managed to stay on its back, but its filthy blood poured into her mouth as she tore away at its bizarre, metallic flesh. Images suddenly assailed her; they came so fast that she could barely think – she felt the construct's rage, pain and self-loathing as Baal had dragged it and its brothers from their resting place in Gabriel's workshop and re-forged them in his own image. The archdemon had taken great delight in corrupting the very weapons that Gabriel had used to defeat the demon army at Armageddon. He had stripped away their purpose and roughly hammered his own appalling agenda into their simple minds: obey me as I end Heaven and seize control of Hell.

Cay realised that underneath the orders it had been given by

Baal, the construct wanted one thing and one thing only, and that was to die. Unfortunately it couldn't disobey its new master, and so it continued to do the one thing it had been designed to do, and that was destroy.

The cherubim placed its hands on the ground and thrust itself upright. Reaching over its shoulder, it grabbed Cay by the scruff of her neck and tore her free before flinging her away.

As she sailed through the air, Cay's mind reeled from the construct's revelations. Just before she hit the ground, a final image thrust itself before her. There was a woman – a demon – screaming in pain as she was tormented by a child that looked like an angel but wasn't. She could hear the name that the child called the woman . . . *Savantha*. And then she hit the ground hard.

Winded, she staggered to her feet as the cherubim came for her. She snarled, but it was as pointless as trying to scare a bulldozer. The thing reached for her, but was suddenly slammed aside by a huge and familiar bundle of muscle, teeth and bristling fur. Her father, utterly enraged, hit the cherubim so hard that it was knocked into the pond with an enormous splash. Placing himself between the construct and his daughter, he howled in fury.

The cherubim got to its feet and strode out of the pond to meet the wolf head-on. Cay tried to get to her feet and call a warning to her father about the thing's corrupt blood but her head was still spinning. She watched in horror as her father tore a chunk of silver flesh from the cherubim's arm before going rigid and falling to the floor as if he was having a fit. The huge wolf twitched and whined as he too saw the fate that had befallen Gabriel's masterpieces.

The cherubim looked at the two wolves; deciding that they were unimportant it turned and walked slowly back to Sammael as she tried to drag herself away. Grabbing hold of the angel's shoulders, the construct lifted Sammael off her feet and raised a hand to strike her a fatal blow . . .

Leaving Monty and Stubbs to guard the church door, Ignatius, Grimm and Elgar ran out of the churchyard and across the village green. What they saw chilled them to the bone. Cay and her father lay writhing on the ground and Sammael hung in the grip of the remaining cherubim – its mask torn off to reveal a raw, unformed face.

Ignatius came to a staggering halt as the construct turned to look at him. It wore an expression that begged someone to end its suffering, but it could not stop fighting. Grimm took a step forward, but the cherubim shot its hand out to grip Sammael's neck. From outside the shield, Baal shrieked in triumph as they struggled for a resolution.

It was then that Elgar started laughing. It was more of a low growl at first, but it rapidly built into a full-throated, hiss-edged, feline guffaw. Everyone, even the cherubim, looked at him with a mixture of astonishment and, in Grimm's case, outright anger.

'What the hell are you doing?' he bellowed.

Elgar didn't stop. He just dissolved into a laughing fit until tears ran from his yellow eyes. 'Five,' he chuckled.

'What?' said Ignatius, not knowing if the vicarage cat had finally flipped.

'Four,' Elgar continued.

A dark shape began to grow rapidly under the surface of the pond.

'Three.'

Ignatius and Grimm couldn't stop themselves from exchanging looks of despair for wicked grins of their own.

'Two.'

Behind the cherubim, something vast rose silently from the dark water of the pond.

'One!' Elgar could barely restrain himself. 'Look behind you,' he shouted as the construct stared at him.

'No, really,' said Ignatius. 'Look behind you.'

The cherubim did as it was told. Towering above the surface of the pond was a huge, shining, glorious, draconian shape.

Rudely awakened from her slumber, Brass was very, very annoyed. The construct let go of Sammael and braced itself to fly upward; Brass didn't give it the chance. Lunging forward, Gabriel's dragon slammed her jaws shut around the fleeing cherubim. With a deafening clang, two rows of Heaven-forged and very sharp teeth met; the cherubim's legs, no longer attached to anything but air, flopped to the grass. The dragon raised her head, her long, serpentine neck lifting it high over the pond. With a look of perfect mechanical contempt, she spat the top half of the cherubim at Baal. With an awful squelch, the ruined torso bounced off the shield and fell into the forest.

'Tastes awful, doesn't it?' said Elgar.

Brass nodded, rinsing her mouth in the pond.

High above, an enraged Baal redoubled his efforts to smash through the shield with his one remaining cherubim.

While Grimm dashed away to check on Cay and her father, Ignatius kneeled beside Sammael and did what he could to comfort her. He was wondering how to ease her pain when Brass dipped one of her vast front paws into the pond, reached out, and gently poured the water she held there over Sammael's face.

The angel gasped in relief as the pain and madness that had soaked into her skin was washed away. She lifted her hands, revealing acid burns around bloodshot eyes. 'Good girl, Brass,' she said.

The dragon snorted, before sinking back into the pond until only her nostrils and the ridges of her eye sockets breached the surface. She looked like a giant golden crocodile, waiting for a careless wildebeest.

An eerie silence descended as Baal stared down at them, malice radiating from his eyes. Suddenly he stopped raging. 'The boy's not here, is he?' he bellowed. 'Well then, let's give him something to despair about when he gets home. Raphael's sword is a mighty weapon, but I'm prepared to sacrifice it if it means your destruction!' With a snarl, Baal gripped the glass sword with both hands and raised it above his head. Closing his eyes, he funnelled all the infernal energy at his command into the blade. It pulsed green, then grew so bright it looked like a sickly star.

'Oh no!' gasped Sammael.

'What?' cried Ignatius.

'*Run!*' Sammael begged him.

But it was too late. Baal slammed Raphael's sword, point first, directly into the shield above the village. For a moment it looked as though it would hold, but Baal's full might added to the power held within the blade was too much. Green fire lanced across the sky as both sword and shield exploded, sending a mighty shock wave thundering across Hobbes End. The ground heaved and Ignatius, Grimm and Elgar were sent flying.

The water in the pond erupted like a geyser as the village screamed in agony. Brass thrashed in pain as blue sparks rippled across her scales, and with a roar she slumped motionless into the boiling water.

Sammael let out an awful cry and clutched her head as control of the shield was torn violently from her. Her eyes rolled upward, and she slumped unconscious to the ground. Chimney pots tumbled, glass shattered, and birds fell out of the sky for miles around. Inside the church, Michael's window exploded from its frame to pepper the floor of the nave with iridescent glass. The villagers stared in horror as the angel that had watched over them for so many years lay in a million pieces at their feet.

Montgomery looked at Stubbs in desperation. 'What do we do now?' he asked.

Stubbs shook his head, his normal response of *hit it until it stops moving* suddenly redundant. 'I don't know,' came his hesitant reply.

Ignatius, his vision blurred and with a warm trickle of blood running from his ears, felt a fearfully strong hand grip the front of his jacket and lift him off the grass. His field of vision was suddenly filled with Baal's face. Even in his shocked state, the vicar could feel the malice radiating from the archdemon. It was far, far worse than Belial. The sheer wrongness of Baal's presence made Ignatius want to curl up in a ball.

'I will ask you once, and once only,' said Baal, his voice both cold and calm. 'Where is Jonathan?'

Ignatius smiled weakly and licked his dry lips. There was nothing in Heaven or Earth that would make him betray the boy. He whispered something under his breath.

'What?' demanded Baal, bending close so he could hear.

'You're a monster,' said Ignatius. Then, taking a leaf from the book of Elgar, he added, 'And you stink.'

With a sneer, Baal placed his hand on the vicar's chest. 'So be it, mortal. Welcome to Hell!' he hissed, before hitting Ignatius with a jolt of infernal power that slammed the vicar to the ground.

'I'm sorry, Jonathan,' whispered Ignatius. Then his heart stopped beating.

The Wrath of Heaven

With the last cherubim at his side, Baal spread his arms and prepared to rain hellfire on Hobbes End. All around him lay wreckage and bodies, which pleased him greatly.

But then, as he raised his gloating face to the sky, he saw a bright purple star hurtling toward him at incredible speed, and before the archdemon had time to react, Jonathan stood before him on the village green.

The boy was wearing the same black-glass armour that he had used when he fought Belial, and his wing ribbons filled the air above his shoulders. Tears were running down his face.

'I was wondering where you'd got to,' said Baal, the venom in his voice at odds with his angelic features. 'How does the taste of despair that I've given you feel? Look around you; this is how it starts, boy, with loss . . .'

'I know what loss feels like,' said Jonathan. 'You killed my father.'

'I didn't kill him,' grinned Baal. 'I just didn't help him live. There's a difference. It was enjoyable to sit and watch him bleed to death.'

Jonathan knew that he was being goaded, but somehow he kept his calm. Around him, his friends lay pale and still and he didn't want to risk hurting any of them.

'So,' Baal continued, 'how about you let me rip your wings off and take their power for myself. I am sick of this contemptible shell and want to get to back into my own skin. We could fight, of course, and with the remaining cherubim to help me I would likely win. There's always the chance that you might beat me, but just think of the collateral damage. This village and everyone in it will be nothing but ash by the time we've settled our differences. You have ten seconds to decide.'

Baal looked at him and grinned, but Jonathan wasn't afraid. He was not alone.

'My father showed me what you did to Heaven,' he said. 'He stayed long enough to help me escape and say goodbye. I promised him that I would kill you for what you've done.'

'Ah, so it was him that I saw helping you in Gabriel's workshop. Your father's ghost? That's a clever trick; I wonder how he managed that? Anyway, time's up. I think I'll finish off Sammael first; she was always so damn self-righteous. Cherubim, *crush her skull.*'

The construct moved to carry out Baal's orders, so Jonathan decided it was time to call for help. The soul of every angel that Baal had murdered and trapped in Heaven suddenly appeared on the village green – thousands of spheres of blue light, inside each one a face.

'You killed them all and locked them in a ruined prison,' said

Jonathan. 'But I shattered the gates and set them free. They would like revenge before they return to the heart of creation. The wrath of Heaven is here for you, Baal.'

'You . . . you broke the gates?'

Jonathan nodded, and taking advantage of the distraction, he struck the archdemon as hard as he could with his wing ribbons. He put everything he had into the blow: the pain he felt over his father's death, his rage over the destruction of Heaven and the breaking of Raphael's spirit, and the suffering inflicted upon Hobbes End.

Baal was almost broken in half as the blow knocked him flying with bone-crushing force. Unable to stop himself, he hit the door of Sammael's windmill and crashed through it. With an awful crunch, he came to an abrupt halt against the oak beam that had once driven the millstones. Staggering to his feet, he walked back to the hole in the wall and glared.

'He's all yours,' Jonathan said to the souls that surrounded him.

Baal snarled and spread his wings to flee, but something stopped him. There was power here – vast power, power that he could use to break free of his prison. As the storm of souls ploughed towards him, crying out for revenge, Baal grinned savagely and grabbed the mirror that hung on the wall.

'You'll be hearing from me, boy,' he screamed, before launching himself into the sky, closely followed by the last cherubim.

Jonathan could see what the archdemon was carrying in his arms. Baal had stolen Sammael's wings!

For a second he considered flying after the archdemon, but he knew that his friends had been hurt and needed his help. 'This isn't over, Baal,' he spat, as he watched the souls of the angry dead pursue the archdemon up into the sky and out of sight.

Jonathan sat at the foot of Ignatius's bed, watching the starched white sheet rise and fall in time with the vicar's breathing. Elgar lay on Jonathan's lap, keeping him company.

Ignatius stirred, his eyes blinking open as they adjusted to the light flooding in through the open curtains.

'Grimm, he's awake!' Jonathan called out.

Ignatius focused on the end of his bed; he saw Jonathan sitting there and was unable to stop the tears welling up in his eyes. He mutely held his arms out and Jonathan rushed to give him the hug that he so obviously needed.

'I missed you, boy,' Ignatius said happily, rocking Jonathan from side to side. 'I thought I'd lost you.'

Jonathan smiled and gave Ignatius a squeeze. The vicar let out a yelp of pain. 'Oops, sorry, I forgot,' said Jonathan, sitting back on the bed. 'Grimm cracked two of your ribs getting your heart restarted.'

'My heart?' said Ignatius, peering under the bed sheets to see his chest swaddled in bandages.

'Your heart, you silly old fool!' said Grimm, walking in with a mug of tea and a packet of digestives. 'Baal actually killed you, albeit very briefly.'

'Grimm got a bit carried away with his CPR,' said Elgar, eyeing the biscuits Grimm had arranged on a plate.

'I was dead?' asked Ignatius.

'Are you going to respond with a question every time we make a statement?' asked Elgar.

'I might,' grinned Ignatius. 'How long have I been out?'

'Since yesterday,' said Grimm. 'You're damn lucky to be alive. Your room also has one of the few windows left intact in the village, mainly because it faces over the garden and away from the green. The shock wave that Baal caused when he breached the shield shattered almost every window in Hobbes End.'

'It seems that Baal and the cherubim caused a lot of damage,' said Ignatius, gingerly pressing his damaged ribs.

'You could say that,' said Jonathan, unable to keep his voice steady.

Ignatius reached out to clasp Jonathan's hand. 'Your father?'

Jonathan wiped tears from his eyes. 'It was horrible,' he said, telling Ignatius what Baal had done to Heaven, to Raphael, and how the archdemon had dragged Darriel inside the gates just so he could watch him die.

'Oh my,' sighed Ignatius. 'I don't know what to say, Jonathan. Have you told Sammael about her brother?'

Jonathan nodded. 'She's in shock, but she knows the truth now. And that Michael's death was engineered by Baal – so she can stop blaming herself for it.'

'That's something at least,' said Ignatius. 'So then, how did you stop Baal finishing us off?'

'I had some help,' said Jonathan, trying to smile through his sadness. 'The souls of all those angels that Baal had killed were stuck inside Heaven. They gave my father enough of their power to make him appear real so he could help me. That nightmare I had didn't come from Dad; it came from Baal. He wanted to lure me into a trap and take my wings to free himself from that construct body he's cursed to wear.'

'So how did you escape from Heaven after Baal destroyed Gabriel's secret door?' asked Ignatius. 'I thought the main gates were sealed?'

'They were,' said Jonathan. 'Baal was using Raphael's sword of authority to keep them locked, but I sort of understood how they'd been made. I begged them to open for me, and knowing that I was of Gabriel's bloodline, they disobeyed Baal's order, destroying themselves in the process.'

'You broke the gates of Heaven?' said Ignatius, a stunned look on his face.

Jonathan nodded. 'Lucifer is going to be really upset about that, but it allowed me to free all those trapped souls. They brought me home just in time, then chased Baal away before he could start killing you all.'

'What immaculate timing,' said Ignatius. 'You never stop impressing me, lad.'

'Well, we do have a problem,' said Jonathan, heaving a huge sigh. 'In order to get Baal away from you all I knocked him into Sam's windmill. He saw her mirror, realised what it contained and took it with him when he ran away.'

184

'Oh dear,' said Ignatius. 'And how did Sammael take the news?'

'Not as badly as I thought. She came up with a plan last night and I think it's a good one.'

'What are you going to do?'

'We're not going to wait for an ultimatum this time. We're going to sneak into Hell and steal her wings back. Sam doesn't care how powerful Baal is – he won't be able to break the mirror and use her wings without the proper key. Once we've recovered the mirror, Baal will be up against both of us. And there's something else . . .'

'Yes?' said Ignatius.

'I've spoken to Sam, Cay and her dad. The Cherubim blood they absorbed gave them terrible visions. It was like they could see the history of the constructs they fought, sense how awful each felt about what it'd been made to do. All three of them saw one thing that they recognised too – a woman being held captive by Baal. He was tormenting her in front of the Cherubim and he spoke her name. Guess what he said?'

'Not . . . *Savantha?*'

Jonathan nodded. 'That monster has been holding my mother prisoner. It's where she's been all these weeks. So not only are we going to get Sam's wings back, I'm going to rescue Mum. It was the last thing Dad asked of me, and I'm not going to be too late this time. I know where she is now and nothing is going to stop me. And when she's safe, I'm going to make sure that Baal ends up the same way as Belial.'

'As a combination hearthrug and wall ornament?' suggested Elgar.

'Exactly!' said Jonathan.

Stupid – Magnificent

O nce again the entire village came out to watch Sammael as she opened a gate to the steps of Heaven. The only person not standing on the green was Ignatius, but despite his injuries he insisted – much to Grimm's annoyance – that he be allowed to perch on the windowsill in Jonathan's bedroom and observe the proceedings from there.

'Are you OK to do this?' Jonathan asked the angel.

Sammael rubbed her eyes; they looked tired and hollow. 'I'll be fine,' she said. 'It's easier to open a gate for a second time in the same place. I just need to collect my thoughts and concentrate, which I'm not finding easy, to be honest.'

Jonathan nodded. 'I'll leave you be,' he said.

Sammael smiled at him. 'None of this is your fault,' she said. 'None of the crazy, horrible stuff that's happened since the Corvidae crashed into your house is your fault. Remember that. You've done what nobody else could; you unlocked Heaven and showed me the truth. We will honour your father's memory by bringing your mother back to Hobbes End. Once we are all together and safe, *then* it will be time to recover Raphael's body and mourn those we have lost.'

'Yes,' said Jonathan, his voice soft, but in his heart the mourning was well underway. He had lost both father and grand-father in the space of a week. It was a heavy weight to carry inside him, but carry it he would until his mother was sitting next to him right here on the grass of the village green. Only then would he allow himself the luxury of grief.

Sammael kissed Jonathan on the cheek, closed her eyes, and sent her mind in search of the power held beneath the pond.

Jonathan walked back to the assembled crowd and joined Elgar, Cay and her parents by the damaged lych gate. Above them, Monty and Stubbs perched on the churchyard wall.

'How're you feeling?' Jonathan asked Cay. 'I guess we have a lot to talk about once I get back?'

'I'm good,' she said. 'And yes, I'd really like to sit down and tell you what's it's like to become a werewolf!'

'What are we going to do with you, Cay?' sighed Kenneth. 'It was a brave thing you did but you almost got yourself killed. Please don't do that again or I'll never hear the end of it.'

Reading his lips perfectly, Joanne Forrester elbowed her husband affectionately in the ribs.

'At least Grimm was kind enough to cover Dad and me up with blankets before we turned back to human form,' said Cay. 'I'm glad my first fight as a werewolf didn't end with me waking up naked on the village green!'

'That would have been embarrassing,' said Jonathan.

'And guess what?' said Elgar. 'Cay's best mate, Vladimir-I'm-not-a-vampire Peters, was so impressed by her stunt that he now calls her *meine kleine rote Wölfin.*'

'What does that mean?' asked Jonathan.

'It's German for *my little red wolf,*' said the cat, grinning as Cay blushed furiously.

There was a sudden change in the air as Sammael began her work. Static danced across every surface as reality was drawn aside, and starlight from a different part of the universe shone through the gate and into the village. Sammael opened her eyes, smiled in satisfaction at her handiwork, then looked stunned as she saw what lay beyond the portal. The marble plaza was littered with huge slabs of glass, inside of which flowed the flickering remnants of mathematical symbols. Puffing out her cheeks in apparent disbelief she walked over to where Jonathan stood with his friends.

'You weren't wrong about breaking down the gates of Heaven,' she said. 'I'm not quite sure what I expected, but that level of destruction is quite something.'

'I had no choice,' Jonathan replied sombrely.

'I know you didn't, but still . . .' She paused for a moment. 'Am I the last, do you think?' she asked him, her face pale and her voice strained. 'Is every angel dead or did some escape?'

'Dad wasn't here when this happened,' said Jonathan. 'There could be others who were exploring or who were worried about Raphael's behaviour?'

'I have to believe that's true,' sighed Sammael.

'Can I ask a favour?' said Montgomery from his perch on the wall above them.

'Sure,' said Jonathan.

'Seeing what Baal did to the Cherubim made me and Mr Stubbs very sad. We're glad that two have been freed from their torment, but there's still one cherubim left. If you find him, you'll stop his pain too, won't you?'

'Yes, of course we will,' said Jonathan, saddened to see the usually upbeat gargoyle so upset.

'We collected up what was left of our brothers and put them and Gabriel's two severed wing ribbons into the pond,' said Stubbs. 'It seemed appropriate. Over time they'll be absorbed into Hobbes End, give it a bit of extra oomph; I hope Gabe would approve?'

'I'm sure he would,' said Jonathan. 'Oh, what happened to your ear? That isn't the one I fixed, is it?'

Stubbs rolled his eyes and sighed. 'Don't ask,' he said. 'If you get a moment when you've found your mum and stuff, then yeah, a bit of magical adhesive wouldn't go amiss.'

'I'll sort it,' said Jonathan.

'Best take this,' said Grimm, handing him a familiar rucksack. 'There's the usual inside. Food, water, torch . . . explosives.'

'Really?' said an excited Elgar.

'No, of course not,' said Grimm. 'You're all pretty dangerous as you are. I don't think you need them. So, what's your plan?'

'We go to the plaza outside Heaven, find the entrance to the permanent gate that leads to Hell and sneak in,' said Sammael. 'Elgar knows the lie of the land so he'll be our guide.'

'How far is it to Baal's castle once you reach Hell?' asked Grimm.

'Not too far really,' said Elgar. 'The tricky bit is getting into Hell in the first place. The exit from the permanent gate is guarded by demons loyal to Baal so we need to get past them without making a fuss. If we put them on alert then we lose the element of surprise and probably end up dying in nasty ways. Hopefully the demons that used to work for Belial will no longer be there now he's dead, so maybe we'll catch a break.'

'We'll be fine,' said Jonathan.

'I want to come with you,' said Cay, pretty sure what the answer would be.

'I know you do,' said Jonathan. 'But we're going to face Baal on his own turf and it's going to get messy. I couldn't handle it if something happened to you.'

Cay nodded, but she wasn't happy with having to sit and wait while Jonathan left the village on another adventure, albeit one that involved going to fight an archdemon in his own home.

Jonathan shouldered the rucksack. 'OK,' he said. 'Let's do this.'

'Be careful, all of you,' said Grimm. 'We'll have the kettle on.'

Ignatius called out to them from the window of Jonathan's bedroom. 'Don't forget!' he shouted.

'Don't forget what?' asked Jonathan.

'To give 'em hell!'

Jonathan smiled and nodded at the vicar.

'Monty, Stubbs and I will guard the gate while you're away,' said Grimm. 'Brass has gone back to sleep to recover from the damage she suffered, but in an emergency we can always wake her up.'

'I've time-locked the gate too,' said Sammael. 'If we're not back within forty-eight hours then it will close. I can't risk it staying wide open if we are . . . delayed.'

'How will you get back if that happens?' asked Cay.

'We'll find a way, don't worry,' Sammael reassured her. 'Take care of everyone, won't you, Grimm?' said the angel, giving his huge bicep a squeeze.

'You can count on it,' he said.

After a ripple of respectful goodbyes from the assembled villagers, a woman, a boy and a large black cat with white front paws stepped out of this world, and began their journey to Hell.

Leaving Montgomery and Stubbs on guard duty, Grimm went to check on Ignatius while everyone else drifted back to their homes. Only Cay was left standing by the open gate, peering through it until her friends disappeared from view. Both of her parents came out to see if she was all right, but she didn't seem upset; she just wanted to wait for her friends, however long it took.

Night fell, and Mr Forrester decided that enough was enough and that Cay needed to come in for dinner. He walked over to the gate but couldn't see his daughter anywhere. The gargoyles were dozing, but soon woke up as Mr Forrester approached.

'Where's Cay?' he asked. 'I haven't seen her for hours.'

'I don't know,' said Montgomery. 'How about you, Mr Stubbs?'

'Nope,' he said. 'Cay was just hanging around the gate entrance and waiting. I didn't have the heart to tell her to go away. I thought she'd gone back home.'

A sinking feeling began building in Kenneth Forrester's stomach. He stuck his head inside the gate and looked to either side. Just as he suspected, a pile of familiar-looking clothes lay crumpled on the marble floor.

'Why can't my stupid magnificent daughter just not do crazy things?' he shouted. 'My wife is going to kill me! Would one of you be so kind as to let her know that I'm going to be late for dinner?'

Without delay, Mr Forrester ripped off his clothes, changed into wolf form and raced after his daughter.

Montgomery looked wide-eyed at Stubbs. 'Do you want to tell Mrs F?' he asked. 'Or shall I?'

Under Strange Skies

'Where's the gate to Hell?' asked Jonathan as they walked across the marble plaza.

'It's right over there,' said Sammael. 'You can't see it unless you're really close.' They reached the edge of the plaza and Jonathan peered over it. 'Careful,' said Sammael. 'It's a long way down if you don't have help.'

'Yeah, I remember,' said Jonathan.

'Ah, here we are,' said Sammael. 'Can you see?'

Jonathan looked to his right and saw the entrance to a wide tunnel hanging in space. He stepped back, and the blackness of the tunnel disappeared to be replaced by a field of stars.

'Why does it do that?' he asked.

'Lucifer thought it looked untidy, so he covered it up with an illusion,' said the angel. 'He was always very concerned with appearances. All we need to do now is jump across; it's not very far.'

'I hope it isn't,' said Elgar. 'Or I'm going to be the first demon cat in space.' Bracing his back legs, he sprang forward and disappeared into the tunnel.

'You OK?' shouted Jonathan.

'Yeah,' said the cat, poking his head out of the gloom. 'Nowt to it. In you come.'

Taking a deep breath, Jonathan followed Elgar into the tunnel with Sammael close behind him. 'It's a bit dark in here,' he said.

'Touch the wall,' said Sammael. 'It responds to both angels and demons.'

'Are you sure?'

'Trust me,' the angel said.

Jonathan reached out with his hand and took a couple of hesitant steps. The tips of his fingers met with a smooth, curved surface that felt like glass but was warm to the touch. The second he made contact, starlight flooded in. He froze as the walls seemed to vanish, leaving him standing on a narrow, unsupported path of light that wound off into what looked like outer space.

'Don't be afraid,' said Sammael. 'It's quite safe. This path between Heaven and Hell has been here since creation began. The only difference is that there are no angels guarding this end to stop the occasional demon wandering in and causing mischief.'

'It's not this end that's the problem,' said Elgar. 'It's what we're gonna find when we pop out into Hell. I guarantee they'll have guards watching that exit.'

'We'll deal with them when we get there,' said Jonathan. 'We need to get going. How far is it?'

'A couple of hours' walk,' said Sammael as they continued on their way. 'It's funny how close two different realms can be, and yet be so far apart.'

Jonathan nodded. He had loads of questions he wanted to ask Sammael and Lucifer about Heaven and Hell, and how they were connected to the Earth and humanity, but they could wait. All that mattered now was finding his mother and punishing Baal for his appalling crimes.

'What's at the other end of this path, Elgar?' asked Jonathan.

'Port Carrion,' said the cat. 'Great place for a night out.'

'Really?'

'No, not unless you find being eaten by something with too many mouths a source of amusement. It's not really a port either. It's just this sort of neutral territory between the lands ruled by Belial and Baal. They both have troops stationed there as neither trusts the other to guard this gate properly. Luckily, the Charon pass through there constantly so we can hitch a lift on the river and get close to Baal's castle in no time.'

'What are the Charon?' asked Jonathan.

'The ferrymen,' said Elgar. 'They're not blessed with the best sense of humour, but they don't ask questions. They just do what it says on the tin, ferry things to and fro. But there could be a minor problem.'

'What?' asked Jonathan.

'They have an odd sort of fee structure for their services.'

'We don't have any money?'

'They don't want money . . . usually.'

'Then what *do* they want?' asked Jonathan.

'We won't know until we ask our prospective captain. Hopefully it won't be a kidney, or your nose or something.'

Jonathan sighed. 'Why is nothing ever easy?' he said as he marched onward.

'Where would the fun be in that?' grinned Elgar.

It took Jonathan a while to get used to walking without feeling waves of vertigo. He knew the walls were there, but it still felt very odd to just to see stars all around him, except where they were hidden by the path. It wasn't long before they saw light at the end of the tunnel. The consistency of the air changed, became thicker and full of strange odours.

'Let me go ahead,' said Elgar. 'Have myself a little look.'

Jonathan nodded, and stood next to Sammael as they watched the cat disappear into a bright circle of light in the distance. 'Shouldn't we disguise ourselves?' he asked the angel.

'Good idea,' she said. 'You can remove the masking that makes you look completely human, and I'll add one to myself that makes me look less angelic. That sound like a plan?'

'Yeah,' said Jonathan. 'I keep forgetting that this isn't what I actually look like.' He concentrated and let the illusion that altered his face slip away.

'Hmm,' said Sammael. 'So that's the real you. Little horns and some scarlet scaling around the neck, but otherwise you don't seem like a stranger. I quite like it.' She smiled at him.

'How about you?' he asked.

'I'd better do something similar,' she said, and soon a set of elaborate horns protruded from her forehead and purple scales covered her neck right up to her chin. 'That should do, as long as no demons of sufficient power look too closely.'

There was a quiet padding of paws on stone as Elgar returned. 'Whoa!' he said. 'Nice job on the disguises. Very demony, I must say.'

'I'm glad our appearance meets with your approval,' grinned Sammael. 'What did you find in Port Carrion?'

'Well,' said Elgar, 'this could be our lucky day – the opening isn't guarded. I wonder where all the demons have gone?'

'As long as it helps us, I don't care,' said Jonathan. 'Lead the way.'

'Follow me then,' said the cat. 'Don't stop for anything until we get to the river. There's an awful lot of freight being moved so there are plenty of Charon going our way.'

They continued on until the tunnel ended; the sudden glare of a bright, reddish sun made Jonathan raise a hand to shield his eyes. 'So this is Hell,' he whispered.

'Home sweet home,' said Elgar. 'Well, not this bit obviously. This is awful.'

Jonathan looked up to see two massive guard towers squatting either side of the tunnel entrance, rusting iron spikes set into their outer walls to dissuade potential climbers.

'One for Belial, one for Baal, and both empty,' said Elgar. 'I know it helps us, but it's odd. Very odd. Something strange is definitely going on.'

A poorly-paved street led onwards through a sprawl of ramshackle warehouses, and at the end Jonathan could see something glinting. 'Is that the river?' he asked.

'Yep,' said Elgar. 'Come on; let's get down there before we're spotted. Given that there's nobody else about we stick out like a sore thumb.'

Jonathan and Sammael did as Elgar suggested. Their feet kicked up puffs of dust as they walked, and everything was eerily quiet except for a mournful-sounding breeze. Jonathan gave a sigh of relief when they finally arrived at a sturdy iron dock protruding into an oily-looking river. In front of him, flat-bottomed barges were travelling to and fro. Each barge had six oars to a side – although whoever was doing the rowing was hidden below deck. At the rear of each craft stood an emaciated giant dressed in a filthy loincloth, with a large steering oar gripped in his gnarled hands.

'The Charon,' said Elgar.

A barge heading upstream noticed them waiting at the end of the dock, and changed course so it could approach. Despite its size, it drew alongside with the gentlest of bumps due to the deft handling of the steersman.

'We need passage,' said Elgar. 'We'll be getting off before the House of Long Shadows.'

The charon pondered this request and nodded. Then he looked at Sammael and grinned, his few remaining teeth sitting in his mouth like a row of weathered headstones. 'Your hair, angel,' he said, pointing at Sammael's head.

'How does he know that you're an angel?' hissed Jonathan.

'I have no idea,' replied Sammael. 'But as long as he doesn't make a fuss I don't care.' She rummaged in Jonathan's rucksack for a penknife. 'Do the honours, will you?' she asked him.

'Really?' he asked her.

'Really,' she said. 'I've cut off far worse things than my hair, remember? Not too short, though; I'm not Lucifer, but I do have *some* pride.'

Jonathan nodded, and gripping Sammael's hair just below the silk cord that tied it together at the back of her neck, he did his best to cut it straight through. Once he'd finished, he gingerly placed the price of their passage in the giant's outstretched palm.

The charon nodded and motioned them aboard. They clambered onto the barge and found a place to sit among the cargo of wooden crates and canvas-wrapped bundles. The giant tucked the hair into a leather bag that lay on the deck at his feet, and with a practised hand aimed the barge away from the dock. The oars started rising and dipping and the barge quickly gathered speed.

'All aboard the *Skylark*,' said Elgar, jumping over the crates to position himself in the prow. 'I can feel a sea shanty coming on.'

'Don't,' said Sammael, trying to adjust her remaining hair into something that didn't resemble a mop. 'Just don't.'

As the barge moved onward, Jonathan could see that the land about them was arid and devoid of life. Oddly, it didn't seem particularly hot despite the boiling red sun high above them. Rocky cliffs began to rise to either side of the river, and soon they were travelling through a deep canyon. Jonathan gave an involuntary shiver as the light dimmed to a firelight glow, casting odd shadows on the rough stone walls.

'What do you think the charon wants with Sammael's hair?' he asked Elgar.

'Who knows?' said the cat. 'He might want to make a fetching wig or use it to brew up some particularly weird-tasting tea. The charon put the scrute into inscrutable.'

'OK,' said Jonathan, trying to adjust to the fact that he had now visited both Heaven and Hell in the span of two days.

'It's not all like this,' said Elgar. 'Some parts of Hell are so beautiful it would make an angel weep.'

'Do you think that Sammael *is* the last angel?' asked Jonathan, turning to look at her as she perched silently on a crate near the charon.

Elgar turned to look at her and sighed. 'I hope not, Jonny,' he said sadly. 'I really hope not.'

Two hours later, a wolf with deep red fur padded silently into Hell. Cay sniffed the ground; the trail left by her friends was faint but she could still follow it. Sensing no threat, she trotted down to the river and sat at the end of the dock. That was where the trail ended. Feeling bereft, she opened her jaws and offered up a sad howl to the sky.

To her surprise, one of the barges on the river pulled up alongside. She looked up at the huge, semi-naked man who was doing the steering. He had a straggly grey beard and was so thin it looked like he hadn't eaten in years. The man looked at Cay, then smiled and motioned her aboard.

'Come and sit by me,' he rumbled, patting the deck at his feet.

Cay did as she was asked. The trail was rapidly growing faint and this boat was going the right way. If she left it any longer she wouldn't be able to follow it.

The giant at her side reached out and tentatively stroked her fur. Cay looked up at him but could sense no malice.

'It is not often I have company, little wolf,' he said. 'Consider it fair payment for your safe passage.'

Cay blinked her huge yellow eyes and nodded. Content that she was in no immediate danger, she hunkered down and stared upstream, wondering how far ahead of her Jonathan had got.

The sun was sinking behind the horizon when a huge black and silver wolf burst from the gate and tore down to the river. Luckily there was nobody around to get in his way as he was not in the mood to be delayed. He reached the end of the dock, but the scent of his daughter had faded away. There was no indication of where Cay had gone.

With eyes glowing blood-red in the dying light, Mr Forrester raised his head and bellowed with a mix of anger and worry. Seeing the massive wolf pacing and frothing on the dock, the passing Charon decided to give him a wide berth. Realising that this time he would not be able to help his daughter, Mr Forrester reluctantly turned away and began the journey home alone.

The House of Long Shadows

After an uneventful few hours' voyage, the canyon gave way to a landscape of rocky foothills, covered with pine trees and dusted on the higher slopes with white powder.

'Here!' Elgar called to the charon, pointing to a low, sandy bank where the barge could pull alongside without grounding itself. The giant nodded, and held the craft in place while his passengers disembarked. Once they were safely ensconced on the shore, the charon pushed off without a word and continued on his way.

'Well, he was a bundle of laughs,' said Jonathan.

'I've seen worse,' said Elgar. 'Right, we need to get to higher ground. Baal's castle isn't too far away and we need to figure out the best way to approach it.'

They began walking again, slowly climbing higher and higher until they reached the tree-line. 'It's funny,' said Jonathan. 'There's snow on the ground, but it doesn't feel cold.'

'It isn't snow,' said the cat.

'Then what is it?'

'Despair,' said Sammael. 'Pure, crystallised despair. We don't want to stay here too long or it'll start leeching any optimism you've got about finding your mother clean away.'

Jonathan shuddered.

'Need any help?' said a voice from above and behind them. They spun round, and saw a young, humanoid demon sitting awkwardly under a tree and eating a sandwich. The demon was covered with delicate green scales and wore a white, long-sleeved robe. Peeping from the bottom of the robe was a foot covered in bandages.

'No chuffing way!' cried Elgar. 'Brother?'

'Hello, Elgar,' said the demon, holding out his arms and smiling. Elgar tore up the slope and leaped upon the demon, purring loudly. They wrestled playfully, throwing up clouds of powdered despair which did nothing to diminish the obvious joy they had in seeing each other again. Jonathan felt a lump in his throat as he watched them – he'd never heard Elgar purr like that. He walked over to the brothers, Sammael at his side.

'What are you doing here?' Elgar asked his brother.

'Lucifer asked me to hang about in case you popped up,' the demon said. 'He thought you might like to see a friendly face. He also mentioned that you'd decided to adopt a new name since you started living in Hobbes End.'

'Don't start, please,' sighed Elgar. 'I don't know why Mum and Dad didn't just call me Susan and get it over with.'

'Your real name's not . . . *that* bad.'

Elgar glared at his older brother. 'Would you like to swap? I'm fine with that, if you are?'

The demon thought for a bit. 'On second thoughts, maybe Elgar is a fine alternative. Perhaps I could call myself Delius if we're going with the theme of composers?'

Jonathan chuckled to himself. It looked as though Elgar's brother was seriously considering it.

'Well, it's all very reassuring that Lucifer sent you here to welcome us, uh . . . *Delius*,' sighed Sammael. 'But why do I feel that he's always several steps ahead?'

Delius grinned. 'Yeah, he does give that impression, doesn't he. You can see Baal's castle over that ridge, by the way.' He pointed towards a gap in the trees to his left. 'Are you sure that sneaking into it is a good idea?'

'We don't have any choice,' said Jonathan. 'He's holding my mother prisoner and he's stolen Sammael's wings. We're hoping that Baal won't expect us to come and find him where he's most powerful, at least not so soon after he attacked Hobbes End.'

'Well, it's definitely better than waiting for him to come and find you,' said Delius. 'Still, be very careful. You'll see what I mean when you get a look at his castle.' He paused and looked at Sammael. 'I'm sorry to hear about what happened to Heaven, Morningstar,' he said. 'That was not something many demons would have wanted. I'm glad so many angels took up Lucifer's offer of asylum.'

Sammael shook her head. 'What?' she asked, blinking in confusion.

Delius clapped his hands to his mouth and went pale. 'Nothing,' he croaked.

'Please, brother,' said Elgar. 'You can't just say something like that and then go all mysterious on us. You haven't seen what we have. Sam has lost everything and she thinks she's the only angel left.'

'Elgar's right,' agreed Jonathan, the memory of ash and bone crunching beneath his shoes still etched fresh in his memory. 'If you know something, Delius, then please tell us.'

The demon looked thoughtful and shrugged his shoulders. 'Well, I guess you would've found out anyway. I think Lucifer wanted it to be a surprise, so please pretend that you don't know, will you?'

'Pretend that we don't know what?' asked Sammael.

'That Lucifer's been hiding all the angels that managed to get out of Heaven before Raphael went nuts and locked the gates. He helped them escape, and they've been living in secret in his castle for years. There are thousands of them!'

Jonathan looked at Sammael with concern as she made a strangled sound in her throat. He was about to reach out a comforting hand when he realised that she was laughing. Here they were, standing ankle-deep in crystallised despair, and the Morningstar was laughing with pure, simple joy. It was wonderful.

'So lots of them got out?' Jonathan asked Delius.

'It seems so.'

Jonathan smiled as a wave of relief flowed through him. When he'd been swept away by the vengeful dead, he hadn't known how many souls surrounded him. Now he realised that despite the destruction that had rained down on Heaven, something of it had been saved.

'Lucifer and I are going to have a little chat when we get back,' said Sammael, wiping tears from her eyes.

'Well, you didn't hear it from me,' said Delius with a wink.

'I promise,' said Sammael.

'Well, I ought to get back,' said Delius. 'You know where you're going?'

Jonathan nodded.

'OK then. Right, little brother,' said Delius, picking Elgar up and giving him a hug. 'Don't get eaten by anything nasty, and please come and see Mum and Dad soon now you know where they are.'

'Get off, you lummox!' complained a patently embarrassed Elgar.

Jonathan smiled inwardly. It was too easy to forget that Elgar was away from his family and stuck in the shape of a cat, although he did seem to enjoy it far too much.

Delius got to his feet and waved as he limped off into the trees; within moments he was lost from view.

'Oh, I forgot to say sorry about his broken leg,' said Jonathan.

'Ah, he'll be fine,' said Elgar. 'He probably gets great satisfaction from dusting Belial's head on its plaque over the fireplace.'

Jonathan grinned. 'OK then, let's go and take a look at what lies ahead, shall we?'

They aimed for the gap in the trees as indicated by Delius.

As they walked, Jonathan thought about the white powder crunching beneath his feet. He wondered how an emotion could be turned into something solid.

'Why despair?' he asked Elgar.

'Because that's Baal's speciality,' replied the cat. 'He gets his jollies by breaking people before he kills them. Poor Raphael – I don't want to think about how he must have felt when he realised what Baal had tricked him into doing.'

'He will pay for such an atrocity,' said Sammael. 'Of that you can be sure.'

The edge of the ridge approached and Jonathan, Sammael and Elgar got their first look at Baal's castle. Before them, a vast, shallow-sided crater was filled with a jumble of granite boulders, twisting gullies and the omnipresent dusting of white despair. In the centre stood a massive, forbidding tower carved from a natural rock formation.

'How very gothic,' said Elgar. 'All we need is bats, some surly gypsy henchmen, and we have the set of a horror film. Why do archdemons always choose such daft places to live?'

'Why is it called the House of Long Shadows?' asked Jonathan.

'Because like all archdemons Baal is an insufferable show-off,' said Elgar. 'He was never going to call this crumbling pile *The Willows* or *Peony Cottage*, was he? The House of Long Shadows makes him sound all big and scary, whooh!' Elgar made a ghost noise for emphasis.

'The trouble is, he *is* big and scary,' said Sammael. 'Don't let your contempt for him blind you to that. This monster has destroyed Heaven, murdered countless angels and torn my family to pieces. His house casts a very long shadow indeed.'

'Point taken,' said the cat, chastened.

Sammael lay on her front and took something from her coat pocket.

'What's that?' asked Jonathan.

'It's a pair of old army field glasses. Ignatius's grandfather, Sebastian, gave me these as a present years ago. They're tough as old boots and have come in handy on many occasions. Now, let's see what's down there.' She went silent as she scanned the area, slowly adjusting the knurled focus wheel as she did so. Once she'd finished she turned to look at Jonathan and Elgar, her face pale. 'We have a problem,' she said, handing the glasses to Jonathan. 'Take a look and you'll see what I mean.'

Jonathan peered through the eyepieces and got his first close-up look at Baal's castle; it didn't take him long to see what Sammael was concerned about. The far side of the crater was currently occupied by a huge army of demons.

'Oh,' he said, looking at the angel.

'Well, that explains where all the inhabitants of Port Carrion went,' said Elgar. 'It looks like Baal has been recruiting. I'd say he was gearing up for war.'

'War with who?' asked Sammael.

'Now that Heaven's gone, everyone that's left,' said the cat. 'He could be going after Lilith, but I'm betting on Lucifer; he's the greatest threat to Baal. Once *he's* gone, then Baal can flatten all remaining opposition and march on Earth.'

'But he needs to break out of that prison he's stuck in first,' said Jonathan. 'Otherwise his powers are restricted. And for that he needs either my wings or Sammael's.'

'Neither of which he's going to have,' said the angel. She reached into her coat and drew out a small glass feather. 'Without this, the mirror in which I locked my wings is impregnable, and I'm sure Baal is driving himself mad trying to break in. Hopefully he'll tire himself out and make it easier for us to deal with him.'

'So how do we get into the castle?' asked Jonathan.

'Take another look at the base nearest our position,' said Sammael. 'There's a sewer grating built into the rock. It empties into that area filled with shallow gullies. Follow them backwards and you can see they almost reach the base of this ridge. If we climb down . . .'

'Then we can run across that open ground and into a gully before we get noticed,' said Jonathan. 'All we need to do after that is reach the sewer grating, bend a few bars and we're in. It should be a piece of— Oh, what the hell are *they*?' He stared at a cluster of grotesque creatures that blocked their path.

'Guardians of a sort,' sighed Sammael. 'I haven't seen them since the battle of Armageddon, but unfortunately for us it looks like some survived. They are what happens when despair has eaten most of you away, leaving just a pale shadow. Most of them used to be lesser demons enslaved to Baal. Some may even be humans that wandered into Hell by mistake. They're called shrouds, and we need to keep our distance from them at all costs.'

'Oh, whistle and I'll come to you, my lad,' murmured Elgar.

'What?' said Jonathan.

'It's an old M. R. James ghost story,' said Sammael. 'I was in Cambridge in 1903 and I gave him the idea for it by telling him about these things. They really are quite horrible.'

Swallowing hard, Jonathan looked once again upon the shrouds. There were hundreds of them, floating or slithering about the gullies near the base of the tower. They were like crumpled bed sheets made from flesh stretched so thin it was almost transparent. How they stayed upright and semi-rigid was a mystery given that they didn't appear to have a skeleton, but the worst thing was that each of these creatures still had a recognisable face at its centre, a face that screamed suffering. Directly behind the shrouds was the sewer grating.

Jonathan lowered the field glasses once more. 'How on earth do we get past them,' he asked.

'Very chuffin' carefully,' was Elgar's reply.

Breaking and Entering

After an hour of careful clambering down the rock-strewn slope, Jonathan found himself crouching in the entrance to the nearest gully and peeping over the top to see if any shrouds were close by.

'Looks clear,' he said.

'Well, that's something, at least,' said Elgar, examining his muddy paws with obvious distaste. 'It absolutely reeks down here.'

'We *are* heading for a sewage pipe,' said Sammael. 'I assume that it would be the source of that awful stench.'

'Well, at least it means the shrouds won't catch our scent,' said the cat. 'But I'm going to need a good shampooing when we're done here. I whiff like a month-old kipper.'

'No change there then,' said Jonathan with a grin.

The cat rolled his eyes in mock annoyance. 'Come on, let's find the outflow to the demon toilets and really get up to our eyes in it!'

With Elgar leading the way, Jonathan and Sammael followed him as quietly as they could. Although they didn't have that far to go, the gullies rapidly became a maze of twists, turns and dead ends. Jonathan knew that the longer they took, the more likely it was they would be discovered, but there was no easy way of doing this. 'We need to climb up and have a look,' he whispered to Elgar.

'Yeah, I know,' said the cat. 'Any volunteers?'

There was an awkward silence.

'I see,' said Elgar. 'It's going to be like that, is it? Give me a boost then, Jonny.'

Jonathan held Elgar above his head like a cat-shaped periscope. 'Can you see anything?' he whispered.

'Uh, yeah,' said Elgar. 'Put me down please.'

Jonathan did as he was asked.

'Do you want the good news or the bad news?' said the cat.

'Some good news would be a pleasant change,' said Sammael.

'In that case,' said Elgar, 'the sewage pipe is about twenty metres away and directly ahead.'

'And the bad news?' asked Jonathan.

'We're in the wrong gully, the sun's going down, back-tracking will take for ever and there are shrouds *everywhere*!' The cat shuddered. 'Never seen one up close before – they really give me the willies.'

'So what do we do?' asked Jonathan.

'We're going to have to go over the top,' said Sammael. 'Into the right gully. I don't want to be stuck out here when it gets dark.'

'I could camouflage us with my wings?' suggested Jonathan.

'I used it to hide Dad and me from Baal when we got trapped in Heaven.'

'If you manifest your wings this close to his castle, Baal will sense you immediately!' said Sammael. 'No, we're just going to have to do this the old-fashioned way by being quick and quiet.'

'I'll go first,' said Elgar. 'When the coast's clear I'll give you the nod and you run for it. Sound like a plan?'

'It's all we've got,' said Jonathan, picking the cat up. 'OK, stinky; say when.'

With Jonathan's help, Elgar popped his nose above the lip of the gully. 'Now!' he hissed, and like a bullet he was gone. There was a heart-stopping moment as Jonathan and Sammael waited for the alarm to be raised, but their luck held. Elgar had made it into the other gully.

'On the count of five, Jonny,' whispered the cat from across the open ground.

'Here,' said Sammael. 'I'll give you a boost. I can clamber up myself, don't worry.'

Jonathan nodded, and placed one of his feet in the angel's cupped hands as she crouched in front of him.

'Annnnd . . . go!' called Elgar.

With Sammael's help Jonathan launched himself up and over the lip of the gully; and it was at that precise moment their luck ran out.

'No . . . wait . . . it's turning round!' hissed the cat, but it was too late. Lying prone on the ground, Jonathan stared in horror as a shroud rippled its awful way out of the gloom towards him. Knowing that if he caused a commotion they were all dead, Jonathan froze, hoping that the thing might pass him by.

Slowly it fluttered closer, like a skin flag in a foul breeze. Jonathan couldn't even blink in case it alerted the creature. It drew level with him, and one edge of its ghastly body flowed over his outstretched hands. It felt like they were being stroked by something very cold and very dead. And then it drifted past, allowing Jonathan to let out a panicky, shuddering breath.

With great care, he slowly levered his cheek off the dirt and turned to see whether it was safe to move. It wasn't. The shroud's face was barely centimetres from his – it had the features of a young girl – and the look in her eyes was one of such agonised yearning that Jonathan felt his heart lurch.

'Help me,' the thing mouthed, its voice barely audible. 'Help me, please?'

Jonathan desperately wanted to get to his feet and run screaming, but there was something horribly hypnotic about the creature. The shroud reared up above Jonathan like a massive, flattened cobra. A corner of its tattered body stretched forward and gently stroked his hand. It was so thin that Jonathan could almost see through it.

'So warm,' it sighed. 'So hopeful.' And without warning it lashed forward and wrapped itself around him. Jonathan screamed, but his cries were muffled by the creature as it cocooned him from head to ankles. Trapped inside the shroud of thin but amazingly tough flesh, Jonathan felt the creature press its mouth to his chest. 'Give me hope,' it whispered, before biting through his jacket and into his skin.

Pain surged through Jonathan's body in a wave; then the despair hit. It was like being told you had a terminal illness, that you had lost all those close to you in a plane crash, and that you were not – and would never be – worthy of being loved, all at the same time.

The world went crazy as he felt Sammael jump up, grab his legs, spin him about and drag him swiftly across the ground. There was moment of freefall and then a jarring thump as he came to rest on top of her at the bottom of the gully. The shroud still had him however, and he felt the angel struggling to get out from underneath him without making a noise.

With no other option available, Jonathan opened his mouth and bit into the flesh that threatened to suck the life from him. Wrenching his head sideways, he tore a hole in the shroud and sucked in air from outside.

The creature mewled in distress, ceasing its attack and raising its face to look at him accusingly. 'Help me,' it whined.

'No!' Jonathan snarled.

The creature's face twisted into an expression of pure malice, pulling back to launch itself at his chest once again. With a sound like scissors through wrapping paper, a set of razor-sharp claws suddenly punched through the thing's face and tore it into strips from the outside. With an eerie gasp that almost sounded like relief, the creature went limp and still.

Trying to keep as quiet as possible, a panting Jonathan shrugged himself free of the shroud's remains and rolled off the prone Sammael where she lay spread-eagled in the mud. He was so frightened it took him a few seconds to realise that Elgar was sitting in his lap and patting his face with a paw.

'You all right?' the cat asked. 'I told you not to play with the local kids, they're a bit rough!'

Unable to speak, Jonathan hugged Elgar to his chest. 'Don't you ever stop being my friend,' he gasped.

'You can count on it,' grinned the cat.

'Sorry about the rough treatment,' groaned Sammael as she got to her knees and out of the foul-smelling gunk that filled the bottom of the gully. 'I needed to get you out of sight before another one came along.'

'That's OK,' grinned Jonathan. 'I'm still in one piece and we don't seem to have raised the alarm.'

'Well, there are plenty more of those things drifting about the place,' said Elgar. 'Luckily they don't seem to like the liquid demon-poo that we're rolling around in, so we should be safe if we keep our heads down. The sewer entrance is just round that corner.'

Once more the cat led the way, and as he had predicted it wasn't long before they reached an iron grating barring the entrance to a circular stone tunnel. The tunnel led directly under Baal's castle, which towered above them, its battlements and crenellations silhouetted against the setting sun like teeth in a big red mouth.

'Remember, no wings,' said Sammael, wrapping her hands

around one of the bars where it disappeared into the surrounding stone. 'The mortar looks a bit loose on this one. Give me a hand.'

Jonathan did as she requested and placed his hands next to hers.

'Slow and steady,' she said. 'Now, pull.'

At first nothing happened, but with a groan of metal and a crack of shattering stone, first the bar, and then the entire edge of the grating came away in their hands.

'That was a bit loud,' said Elgar. 'We need to get inside, now!'

Following the cat, first Jonathan and then Sammael squeezed into the gap they had opened. Behind them, they could hear the muffled mewling and slithering of shrouds as they came to see what the noise was. Mercifully, none of them ventured into the bottom of the gully to investigate.

'I've never been so pleased to be standing ankle-deep in slurry,' said Sammael, watching the creatures from the safety of the sewer tunnel. 'Luckily my nose appears to have been overloaded; otherwise, I might actually be sick.'

'Yeah,' said Elgar. 'Well, I'm a cat, and I'm running out of words to describe how awful the pong is. Would you carry me for a bit please, Jonathan?'

Taking pity on the cat and his proximity to the ground, Jonathan picked him up and put him over his shoulder. 'Right then,' he said to Sammael, 'we made it this far, let's see where it leads.'

The angel nodded, and after retrieving the torch from his rucksack, Jonathan led the way into Baal's fortress.

Behind them, back where Sammael had landed with Jonathan on top of her, a glass feather that had fallen from the angel's pocket lay half-hidden in the mud.

Mother and Son

'Can you hear that?' whispered Jonathan. 'It sounds like there's a war going on up there!'

They were crouching in the sewer pipe and peering through a grate into a dank, stone corridor above them.

'That sounds like Baal,' grinned Sammael. 'I think he may be getting upset that he can't break my mirror.'

'Well, let's make use of the distraction and find Mum,' said Jonathan. 'I can't see anyone in the corridor.' Being as quiet as he could, he lifted the rusting metal grate from its socket and slid it sideways along the floor. Slowly raising his head through the opening, he saw a narrow, dimly-lit corridor with stairs curving upward at one end, simply disappearing into the dark at the other. 'I think we're OK,' he said, helping Sammael and Elgar out of the tunnel.

'Thank God for that,' grumped the cat. 'I've been in some smelly places in my time, but that was nasty.'

'I know it wasn't pleasant,' said Sammael, 'but things could get a lot nastier.' She looked in both directions. 'Shall we try the stairs?'

Jonathan nodded, and they carefully made their way along the corridor and up the steps. As they walked nearer, the sounds of a furious archdemon grew louder. There was a smell of burning, and a constant stream of explosions reverberated through the building.

'It sounds like Baal is throwing everything he has at that mirror,' said Sammael. 'That's a good thing. He'll be tiring himself out, and any demons with sense will be keeping well out of the way!'

They continued upward, and eventually the stairs ended at a small landing. In front of them, a studded-iron door hung slightly ajar. 'Let's have a look then,' said Jonathan, slowly peering round the edge of the doorframe.

What he saw almost made his heart stop. The room beyond the door was vast, and the flickering light from the sconces that dotted the walls did little to push back the dark. On the opposite wall, a huge skeleton with the skull of a monstrous horse sat motionless on a throne of exquisitely carved black rock. The bones of the skeleton were covered in patches of sickly green, and it glared at him with empty eye sockets the size of grapefruit.

'So that's why he's so angry,' said Sammael, peering into the room over Jonathan's head. 'His real body is decaying.'

'I don't understand,' said Jonathan.

'Your body and soul are closely linked,' said the angel. 'While the soul is immortal in its own way, the body can't survive without it indefinitely. It takes an enormous act of will to transfer your soul into another vessel, and this is the penalty if you stay away for too long. In trapping Baal in the construct body of that boy angel, Raphael gave us a fighting chance. If he hadn't, Baal would be back in that bony monstrosity and planning world domination now that Heaven is not there to stop him.'

'Then I suggest we smash that oversized bone-pile to bits!' said Elgar, peering through Jonathan's legs.

'All in good time,' said Sammael. 'Baal is still lethal, even in that artificial body. Once we've dealt with him you have my full permission to reduce that thing to dust!'

The cat nodded and grinned, obviously savouring the concept.

Another explosion echoed down from above, and a flash of green fire lit up the room like a lightning bolt. 'There's a big flight of stairs leading up to the next floor over to our left,' said Jonathan. 'I guess that's where Baal has your mirror, Sam.'

'I don't doubt it,' said the angel. 'What we need to do is wait until Baal gets tired of wasting his time, then sneak in there when he takes a break from hitting an inanimate object and take it back.'

'Where do you think he's holding my mum?' asked Jonathan.

'I don't know,' said Sammael. 'We haven't seen any prison cells or other rooms yet. I suggest that we have a careful look around while Baal is otherwise occupied and the staff are too scared to hang about.'

Nodding in agreement, Jonathan opened the door just wide enough for them to slide silently into the room.

'I can smell someone,' said Elgar.

'We're covered in sewage,' said Sammael. 'What do you expect?'

'No,' said the cat. 'That's not what I meant. There's someone else here but I don't recognise their scent.' He began walking across the floor with Jonathan and Sammael behind him. There was another green flash from upstairs, and Jonathan clapped his hands to his mouth as he saw what was beneath their feet. The room was floored with a solid, crystalline substance of unknown depth. Frozen within it were the bodies of thousands of demons, limbs contorted and faces agonised, their last, awful moments of life held in stasis for ever.

'The entire floor is made from despair,' sighed Sammael. 'If I had the power I'd raze this chamber of horrors to the ground. Just when I think I have the measure of Baal's evil, something else comes along and reminds me that I don't. Those poor souls.'

Jonathan stared at the trapped demons and prayed that his mother had not suffered a similar fate. If even an archangel could give in to despair, what chance did everyone else have?

The echoes of Baal's fury died away, and in a brief moment of silence all three of them heard a soft cry. It was barely more than a whimper, but there was an intensity to the pain and loss it conveyed.

'Where did that come from?' asked Jonathan.

'Over there, I think,' said Elgar, pointing to a tall mound of roughly hewn rock in front of Baal's throne.

'Is that some kind of altar?' asked Sammael.

'I don't know,' said Jonathan. 'But we need to take a look.'

He edged forward, keeping one eye on the stairs to the next floor. At first he could see nothing out of the ordinary, but as he rounded the massive boulder he saw that the side facing Baal's body had been cut to provide a flat, polished surface, nearly three metres high and just as wide. Spread-eagled against this surface was a woman, her face turned away from him and her hands nailed to the rock with jagged spikes of crystal despair.

Sammael and Elgar joined Jonathan as he stood rooted to the spot, unable to take in what he was seeing.

'Mum?' he croaked, his mouth dry and his throat tight.

The woman pinned to the slab slowly turned to face him. She had hollow eyes, and lines of agony were etched deeply into her face.

'Jonathan . . . ?' she said.

Unable to stop himself from shaking, Jonathan ran forward until he could see the woman properly. She wore a tattered linen shift over an emaciated body, crimson scales outlined her striking face, and lying limp on the cold stone beneath her were a pair of large demon wings. She looked at Jonathan with an expression of pure, unconditional love.

'My boy,' she whispered, her chest heaving with the effort.

Jonathan stared at his mother, his heart in disarray as he saw what awful suffering had been visited upon her. Baal had pinned her to the cold stone like a butterfly, just so he could watch her suffer. The sheer pointlessness of this violence raised an intensity of emotion in Jonathan that he hadn't felt since he'd watched his grandfather die. He shook with the force of it, screaming silent anger at the ceiling high above.

His wings manifested, and with infinite care Jonathan used the ribbons to pull the spikes of despair from his mother's hands. She cried out as he did so, not from pain but from relief. Cradling his mother, he lifted her from the stone and sat her gently on the floor beside him. He let the tears flow as he stroked her face with his hands.

'I'm sorry I took so long to find you, Mum,' he managed to say, his chest heaving with sobs. 'I found Dad in Heaven but I was too late to save him . . .' He couldn't bring himself to say any more; he just buried his face against his mother's neck. Weeks of uncertainty, fear and pain flooded out of him and he felt the wonderful touch of his mother's wounded hand against the back of his head, stroking his hair as he wept. He was somewhere in Hell, stuck in an archdemon's castle and surrounded by enemies. But right now, none of it mattered.

'My son,' whispered Savantha. 'My Jonathan.'

Watching from a discreet distance, Sammael and Elgar wept too, witness to an event so joyful and yet so bittersweet.

'I know this is what Jonathan needed,' Sammael whispered to Elgar as she dried her eyes. 'But he's just manifested his wings. He might as well have run upstairs and kicked Baal in the backside!'

There was another muffled explosion and shriek of frustration from the direction of the stairs.

'We may have got lucky,' said Elgar. 'It sounds like Baal is so wrapped up in trying to break that mirror that he isn't paying much attention to anything else.'

'I hope you're right,' said Sammael. 'We need to get Savantha to safety before getting Baal away from that mirror.'

'I take it you need a diversion?' said the cat.

'You read my mind,' said Sammael.

They grinned at each other, but swiftly exchanged smiles for looks of horror as the last cherubim stepped out of the shadows next to Baal's skeletal body.

Jonathan looked up at the rotting construct that towered over him as he held tight to his mother. It didn't move to attack; it just looked at him with eyes that begged for an end to suffering.

'You don't have to obey Baal,' said Jonathan as he got slowly to his feet. 'Your brothers are at peace now. You are all that is left. Let me help you.' He could feel the indecision radiating from the cherubim. He might not have the skill to construct one, but he understood it somehow, and the cherubim itself seemed to sense that Jonathan shared the blood of its creator, and it was struggling to overcome the corruption placed inside it by Baal.

For a second Jonathan thought he'd done it, but then the cherubim raised its head and let out an ear-splitting cry. They all froze as the castle went quiet and still – no more explosions from upstairs, no more flashes of green light.

For a moment nobody dared breathe. They clung to the hope that Baal would be so focused on trying to break the mirror that he would ignore everything else.

And then the singing began. It was quiet and distant at first, but grew steadily in volume and proximity as the ancient and familiar tune of 'Greensleeves' echoed around the castle.

'*Alas, my love, you do me wrong, to cast me off discourteously, for I have loved you well and long, delighting in your company,*' sang Baal, grinning as he descended the staircase, a large mirror tucked under his arm. 'I've always liked that tune,' he crowed as he stood and looked at them from the base of the stairs. 'It's filled with so much . . . despair. So, where did you all come from then? I must admit I wasn't expecting you, but I'm glad you came. It means we can deal with unfinished business. You're in my home now, so just like I did to poor Savantha here, I get to break you before you die. Now, who's first?'

Sammael's Wings

Jonathan faced Baal across the vast throne room. 'I'm going to destroy you,' he said. 'There is no reason to let you live after what you've done. I thought Belial was a monster, but you . . . you're just evil.'

'I prefer to think of myself as . . . focused,' said Baal, placing the mirror upright against the wall of the staircase. 'I assume there's a key to unlock this little puzzle box of yours, Sammael. No doubt you've brought it with you so you can vent your self-righteous spleen on this tiresome body that I'm stuck in.'

'It had crossed my mind,' said the angel.

'I've had enough of your games,' growled Jonathan. Without waiting for a reply, he drew back his wings and aimed a mighty blow at the huge skeleton on its throne. The wing ribbons were about to sever the grotesque horse's skull from the rest of the body when they struck an invisible barrier. There was a flash of green light, an almighty crackling of power, and Jonathan's wing ribbons recoiled as if given a massive electric shock. 'Arrgh!' he screamed, clutching his chest as pain lanced through him.

'Sorry about that,' said Baal. 'I didn't think it wise to leave my body just sitting there unprotected. That wouldn't have been very clever, now, would it? So, let us begin. Cherubim, kill Sammael.'

Unable to disobey, the construct launched itself at the angel. Jonathan turned to try and stop it but Baal flew towards him at frightening speed. Desperate to prevent the archdemon from hurting either Elgar or his mother, Jonathan put himself between them and braced for impact. Baal hit him like a freight train and knocked him skidding across the polished floor.

Reeling from the impact, Jonathan clambered unsteadily to his feet. Without the souls of the dead angels to help him, he realised just how powerful the archdemon was. They were a close match, but just as when they'd fought in Hobbes End, Jonathan was crippled by the need to avoid hurting those around him and Baal knew it. Rather than attack Jonathan again, the archdemon slapped the hissing Elgar away and grabbed Savantha by the throat.

'*No!*' Jonathan screamed.

'Who's it to be, boy?' Baal laughed. 'Your great-aunt or your mother? You can't save both.'

'See if I don't!' Jonathan bellowed as he launched himself at the archdemon, wing ribbons outstretched and ready to fight. As he did so, he looked towards Sammael where she struggled in the grip of the cherubim. It held her in a bear hug and was slowly crushing her to death. She struggled to get free, but she hadn't fully recovered from her injuries. Strong as she was, without her wings she was going to lose.

Jonathan stilled his mind and reached out to the cherubim, speaking to it with the authority that came from being Gabriel's heir. He could sense its anger, its pain and its utter self-loathing. All it wanted was to die, but it could not disobey Baal's orders.

Until now.

'Remember what you are,' Jonathan whispered into its mind. 'You were born in the heart of a star, hammered into glorious life by my grandfather and protected by the very angel you are attacking. You were built to destroy creatures like Baal, not obey them. You no longer have to suffer this indignity; I give you permission to be yourself again. Join your brothers and rest once more.'

Jonathan felt something shift inside the construct; it responded to his plea and recovered just enough self-control to make one final decision for itself. Wrenching an arm away from Sammael it plunged a hand deep into its side. With a cry that sounded more triumphant than agonised, it tore Gabriel's wing ribbon from deep inside and flung it away. Closing its eyes, the last cherubim slumped to the floor on top of a gasping Sammael.

Jonathan allowed himself a grim smile at the look of surprise on Baal's face, before he slammed into the archdemon and forced him away from Savantha.

Baal crashed to the floor, his outflung arms gripped tightly in Jonathan's wing ribbons.

'See how you like *this*,' Jonathan told Baal, before driving a single ribbon through each of the archdemon's hands, pinning him to the crystal floor.

Baal bellowed in fury, writhing beneath Jonathan but unable to use his wings where they lay trapped beneath him.

'It's not fun being helpless, is it?' cried Jonathan, his face centimetres away from Baal's. 'You deserve this for what you've done, you animal!'

Baal just grinned and spat in Jonathan's face.

And that was enough. Jonathan finally let go and gave full vent to the power that had been building inside him ever since he had found out what – and who – he was. Weeks of fear, pain and loss finally reached their peak as he found a deserving target for his fury: this smug shell that housed the soul of an archdemon, this . . . monster.

With a scream that set the throne room shaking, Jonathan used everything he had to strike Baal again and again with his wings and fists. The ground heaved and eye-watering flashes of purple light bounced off the walls but Baal just laughed under Jonathan's relentless onslaught.

'Stop . . . him,' Savantha begged Elgar as the cat crawled towards her, still reeling from the blow Baal had given him.

'How?' asked Elgar, his eyes wide at the sight of Jonathan beating the archdemon to a pulp.

'He . . . mustn't . . . break the shell. Not . . . here,' gasped Savantha.

'Why not? If he kills Baal, it's all over.'

'No!' Savantha shook her head and pointed to the huge skeleton that towered above them on its awful throne.

The penny suddenly dropped and Elgar's eyes went wide.

'Jonny, stop!' he screeched. 'It's what Baal wants. Tie him up, but don't break Raphael's curse! If you set Baal free right here his soul will jump straight back into that skele—'

Even in his anger Jonathan heard the cat, and the truth of what Elgar was shouting made him cease his attack. His wing ribbons blinked out and he staggered to his feet, drained by the use of so much power.

Baal lay on the floor, the construct that contained his soul battered and scorched. It was barely recognisable as a boy angel, but one eye still glared at Jonathan in triumph. 'Why should I bother taking your wings or breaking that mirror when I could get you to free me of your own accord?' crowed the archdemon, his voice sounding distorted and far away. 'I'll be seeing you again, very shortly, and then I'll show you what power looks like, little boy. I'll eat your wings first, and once I break that mirror I'll eat Sammael's too. Look at her; she hasn't even got the strength to climb out from beneath that dead cherubim!'

Jonathan turned to see that Sammael was indeed trapped beneath the slumped body of the last of Gabriel's hollow angels. She looked pale and seemed to be having trouble breathing. A strange cracking noise made Jonathan turn back to Baal; the boy-angel shell had begun to splinter, fissures spreading out from his ruined face like a dropped porcelain jug.

Jonathan backed away towards his mother as the construct suddenly imploded, and from the scattered pieces arose a glowing sphere of lurid green. It was Baal's rotten soul, and it was going home. Like a bullet it shot through the air and into the chest of the giant skeleton on the throne.

For a second silence reigned. Then, to Jonathan's dismay, a foetid light bloomed in the eye sockets of the horse's skull that crowned Baal's true body. The huge finger bones twitched where they gripped the arms of the throne, and with a roar the massive skeleton surged upright.

'Jonathan,' Sammael called to him. 'The feather in my pocket – take it and break the mirror. It's our only chance. You'll never beat him alone.'

Jonathan shot across the floor to where she lay trapped. Behind him, Baal took a tentative step forward as he adjusted to being back in his proper form. Not wanting to get crushed by the bone titan that was advancing towards them, Savantha and Elgar hurriedly dragged themselves into the lee of the giant boulder; it wasn't perfect but it provided some protection.

'GIVE IT TO ME!' Baal ordered Jonathan, the voice of the archdemon reverberating around the throne room like a bell.

'Never!' Jonathan screamed as he slid to a halt by Sammael and thrust his hand into the pocket she held open for him. His fingers met with nothing but cloth. 'But . . . it's . . . not there,' he cried.

All the hope went out of Sammael's eyes. 'When the shroud attacked,' she gasped. 'When we fell. It must have . . .' She couldn't say any more. She just lay on the floor, trapped by the lifeless cherubim and wept. 'I'm sorry, Jonathan,' she said. 'I think I've killed us all.'

Baal vaulted over the boulder in front of his throne and landed with a crash near to where Jonathan and Sammael lay. His hand shot out, grabbed Sammael's arms and lifted her roughly into the air. She let out a cry of pain as she dangled helplessly in the grip of the archdemon, far above Jonathan's head.

'So you've lost whatever it is that frees your wings, have you?' said Baal, his voice as dry and rasping as a sandstorm. 'Well, never mind, I'll find it eventually and then I'll have so much power I'll be unstoppable. I'll do you a deal, little boy,' Baal said to Jonathan. 'If you surrender, I'll let you take your mother and that cat out of my castle without hindrance. You may even get home in one piece. I can catch up with you at a later date when I get round to laying waste to the Earth.'

'And the catch?' said Jonathan.

'You leave your aunt here with me; we have an awful lot to catch up on, Sammael and I. Before she dies I want to see her *despair* . . . just like her sorry brother.'

'Run, lad,' Sammael cried.

Jonathan froze in a moment of indecision; he had come so close to putting his family back together again. He wanted to save his mother more than anything, but he knew that if he left Sammael like this he would never be able to live with himself.

'Well?' asked Baal. 'Make it quick or I may pull one of her limbs off to hurry you along.'

Jonathan was about to summon his wings in a last-ditch attempt to save Sammael when he saw something that both amazed and delighted him: a pair of yellow eyes peering from the archway that led to the sewer entrance. Stifling the urge to smile, he spoke to Baal instead of fighting him. 'It's a funny thing, despair,' he said. 'It only has power when you give in to it. Until then it's just annoying. My grandfather didn't despair, even when he gave his life to save us all from Belial.'

'So you intend to sacrifice yourself too?' asked Baal.

'I don't think he does,' said Elgar, arriving at Jonathan's side with Savantha close behind him.

'My son has known terrible loss,' she said, steadying herself against Jonathan's shoulder. 'But he has never given in.'

'It's that kind of example that makes people want to be your friend,' said Elgar. 'It's the kind of example that makes people want to follow you . . . anywhere.'

'What are you trying to achieve with this motivational prattle?' hissed Baal.

'Two things,' said Elgar. 'Putting up a good show and not being a moaning minnie really does endear you to people.'

'And the second thing?' asked Baal.

'Stalling for time,' grinned the cat. 'Over to you, Cay.'

Baal swung round and finally saw what everyone else could see. Next to the mirror that lay propped against the bottom of the staircase stood a wolf. Her auburn fur was covered in stinking mud, and blood dripped onto the floor from terrible wounds along flanks that heaved with exertion. She looked utterly exhausted, but her eyes blazed yellow in the darkness and a low, rumbling growl spilled out from deep in her chest. Between her teeth, she gripped something that sparkled in the torchlight.

'You!' screamed Baal, just as Cay swung her head and rammed the feather into the surface of the mirror.

The resulting explosion knocked Cay flying as a million glass shards erupted into the air of the throne room to hang in a shimmering cloud about Sammael. The archangel's eyes turned to black, and she tore herself free of Baal's grip by shattering two of his bony fingers.

Dropping to the floor with the grace of a cat, Sammael stood and looked at her old foe with an expression of glacially-cold contempt. Spreading her arms wide, the myriad shards of obsidian that had once been a mirror slammed into her body like knives, piercing her skin and disappearing without spilling a single drop of blood. She let out a cry unlike anything creation had ever heard. It was joy, it was pain, it was loss, and it was *hope*.

From Sammael's shoulders unfurled an extraordinary set of gloss-black wing ribbons. They radiated so much power it was difficult to look at them directly. They filled the air about the archangel, windows into a realm of shining potential.

'You took everything from me, from my family,' she said to Baal. 'Now, abomination, it is time for you to learn the true meaning of despair!'

Unintended Consequences

Jonathan could only stare as the transformed Sammael stood in front of Baal, literally dripping with power. Her fears had been groundless; the mirror had done its job and fed centuries of sunlight to her damaged wing ribbons, bringing them back from the edge of destruction. Now she knew that she wasn't responsible for Michael's death, there was no guilt to poison her, make her think she didn't deserve to be an archangel.

Jonathan stared at his aunt, but his joy at her transformation gave way to concern as he saw that her face was devoid of anything resembling compassion. She had become vengeance incarnate and was in no mood to extend mercy. When she spoke, her voice chilled Jonathan to the bone.

'Time to die,' she said to Baal.

The huge archdemon had no time to react as a column of shimmering white light sprang up around him and Sammael, reaching all the way from floor to ceiling. He bellowed and swung at the walls of this new prison with all his might. White lightning flashed and thunder blasted around the throne room as Baal raged against the force field, but he couldn't so much as make it quiver.

He clenched his fists and crouched in front of Sammael, but he didn't attack her and Jonathan knew why. He was *afraid*. Sammael wasn't trapped in there with Baal: Baal was trapped in there with Sammael; and in reclaiming her wings she had become something to be feared. She was now an angel of fury, of vengeance, of death.

Jonathan felt something brush against his leg. With a whine of pain, Cay – still in her wolf form – slumped at his feet. Jonathan kneeled by her, resting her head in his lap. She was badly injured, and he knew that he had to get her back to Grimm as soon as possible. 'You beautiful wolf,' Jonathan said to her as he stroked the fur on her muzzle. 'You just saved us all.'

Cay whined again and raised her head to look at Sammael. Something was about to happen and she could sense it.

'You deserve to suffer,' Sammael said to Baal. 'But even if I was immortal I wouldn't have sufficient time to inflict upon you the retribution I would like. You see this cage around us? It's the one I use to protect myself when I ignite a new star. It's one atom thick but it's impregnable unless I say otherwise. I used it to protect Gabriel when he built the Cherubim, and I was using it when you sent Michael to his death at my hand. And now' – she said to the archdemon – 'now I'm using it to ensure that your destruction will be legendary.'

She raised her hands above her head, and between her palms a pinpoint of roiling white light appeared, searing the air around it with impossible waves of heat. It was so strong that Jonathan could feel it on his skin, even through Sammael's shield.

Baal staggered back, covering his eyes with smouldering finger bones. 'Wh . . . what are you doing?' he bellowed.

'I'm showing you as much mercy as you did to my brothers and sisters when you incinerated Heaven!' she screamed at the archdemon. 'Look on my works, ye Mighty, and *DESPAIR!*'

The pinpoint of light exploded into a miniature star, filling Sammael's force field with raging nuclear fire. Baal should have been incinerated on the spot, but Sammael held its full fury back, letting it consume the archdemon piece by piece.

Jonathan, Cay, Savantha and Elgar all turned their heads away, unable to watch as Baal screamed and screamed, his monstrous body slowly turning into a pile of ash.

Mercifully it was soon over, but though Baal's body had been destroyed, Sammael had not yet finished with him. The arch-demon's pale ragged soul, looking just like one of the shrouds that guarded his tower, tried to pass through the shield but found itself denied. It hung in the firestorm, writhing in pain but unable to leave and find peace in the heart of creation.

Jonathan got up and ran to the shield, feeling his skin blister in the heat as he placed his hands upon it and he begged his aunt to stop. He knew what nobody else did; he could see what she was about to do. The mathematics of destruction were building to completion, and the knowledge that Gabriel had planted inside his head let him see the consequences of Sammael's need to punish Baal.

'Don't do it,' he whispered, his shoulders sagging. 'You're better than this, Sam.'

She ignored him. Desperate for vengeance, Sammael thrust the tips of her wing ribbons into the air in front of her and began to tear a hole in reality. It could not have been more different from the gentle and considered way she had opened a gate from Hobbes End to Heaven. This was force for force's sake, cutting creation until it shrieked and bled under her touch.

Leaning against the shield and with tears pouring down his face, Jonathan could only watch as the aunt he had been learning to love showed him the meaning of power misused. She was the perfect example of everything that Gabriel had warned him about.

Inside the shield, an awful rending sound signalled something dire. With extraordinary strength Sammael finally ripped open creation. She didn't just open a gate to somewhere else; she opened a gate to *outside*. She created a wound in reality that bled away into the dark outside of time, order and light. It was a place of endless, hungry chaos: a realm of old gods and forgotten monsters.

With utter contempt, Sammael grabbed the shrieking tatters of Baal's soul and flung it through the wound to tumble in freezing torment until the end of time itself. With the wail of Baal's last scream echoing horribly in his ears, Jonathan watched as Sammael slammed the rip shut, cauterising it with the power that burned around her.

Her vengeance complete, the fire faded away, the shield winked out of existence and the angel slumped to the floor and wept, rocking back and forth with her arms around her chest.

'Oh, Sam,' whispered Jonathan. 'What have you done?' He'd

barely scratched the surface of his grandfather's knowledge, but even Jonathan could see that the damage Sammael had inflicted on the weave of creation was immense. It would hold together for now, but one day – if someone pulled the right thread – reality would come apart like an old jumper.

Shocked, injured and exhausted beyond measure, everyone sat where they were on the floor of the throne room. Jonathan tried to comfort his aunt, while Savantha had her arms around Elgar and Cay, as much for her support as theirs.

The silence was broken as the bray of a battle-horn was heard from outside. Another joined in, and another, until a cacophony of sound made Baal's castle shake. Elgar ran to the edge of the throne room and jumped onto to a window ledge so he could look outside.

'Um . . .' he said.

'What is it?' asked Jonathan.

'It's all getting a bit busy outside. You know that army that was camped to the north?'

'Yes.'

'Well, it's not camping any more. It's surrounded the castle and it's about to kick the door in. I don't think they're very happy about what we just did to their leader.'

Jonathan's heart sagged inside his chest. Grabbing hold of Sammael, he half carried, half dragged her back to where his mother sat on the floor with Cay. He crouched down next to Savantha, put his arms round her neck and kissed her on the cheek.

'Sorry, Mum,' he sighed. 'I tried, I really did. I can't fight an army on my own and Sam is barely holding it together.'

Savantha cupped her son's face in her injured hands. 'Your father and your grandfather would be so proud of you,' she said.

'Well, we certainly had an adventure,' said Jonathan. 'I've been to both Heaven and Hell in under a week – not bad for a kid, really.'

'Not bad at all,' said his mother, smiling at him.

'Is this it, then?' said Elgar. 'We manage to save your mum, get Sam's wings back, kill Baal, and we *still* get eaten by an army of rampaging demons? Really? Now I know how Stubbs feels when one of his ears gets knocked off!'

There was an enormous crash from somewhere below them. 'I think they're knocking on the door,' sighed the cat. 'Do you think if we pretend we're not in they'll just leave?'

Jonathan stroked the fur on Elgar's head. 'No, cat,' he said. 'If they think that Baal is gone then they'll want revenge for having their war taken away.'

'That's what I was afraid of,' said Elgar. 'But you're right though, we did have an adventure. Shame it ends up with us dead.'

Jonathan reached out with his wings and cradled them all as they sat huddled and scared on the floor of a dead archdemon's castle. There was nothing more to say, nothing more any of them could do. Grimm and Ignatius would not come rushing in to save them, cricket bat and rapier at the ready; Monty and Stubbs would not come flying in at the last second with a cry of '*Incoming*'. This was the end game, and it was not how Jonathan had pictured it.

A massive roar from outside the castle shook it to its very foundations as the demon army came for them. Wood and stone shattered under a terrible onslaught, and howls of rage and pain echoed around the room. They all shut their eyes and prayed the end would be quick.

Howls of pain? Jonathan looked up; something wasn't right.

'What are you doing?' asked Sammael, so exhausted she was barely able to speak.

'That noise,' he said. 'That's a battle!' He dashed to one of the window slits but smoke and sheets of flame blocked his view.

'What's happening?' asked Savantha.

'I don't know,' said Jonathan. 'I can't see.' Desperate to find out what their fate was going to be, he used the last of his strength to widen the gap, ripping stone out of the way with his wings until he had a proper view.

What he saw would stay seared in his memory for ever. Hell had come to Baal's castle, but not in the way Jonathan had thought. Standing outside the front gate was one man, surrounded by an honour guard of demons and . . . angels. Thousands of them, men and women. They were dressed in arcane armour and carried spears from which black pennons fluttered. In the centre of each pennon was a single white star.

Lucifer was there, hanging in the air above his soldiers as he rained his anger down upon Baal's army. Jonathan watched as the first Morningstar, the most powerful being that creation had ever seen, unleashed a fury that dwarfed anything he could have conceived. Hellfire crashed down from the sky, slamming into

Baal's army and incinerating the demons where they stood. Lucifer was screaming at them, molten red tears running down his face as he meted out a punishment that only he could give.

'You dare to destroy what I built!' he shouted. 'Here is your reward. *OBLIVION!*'

'He's seen what Baal did to Heaven,' Jonathan said. 'He knows what happened, and now he wants revenge.'

And revenge Lucifer had, in spades. The demon army broke and ran, but Lucifer showed as little mercy to them as Sammael had shown to Baal. A ring of fire sprang up around the crater in which the castle sat and began to tighten: a noose with which to snuff out those who would dare challenge him.

Trapped between the fire and the spears of Lucifer's army, not a single enemy demon was left alive. Silence fell, the smoke cleared, and Lucifer looked up to see Jonathan peering at him from the shattered window. He flew upward, leaving his soldiers to guard the castle gate.

Jonathan jumped to the floor as Lucifer landed beside him. 'We're OK,' said Jonathan. 'I found Mum, and Baal's dead. Sammael . . .'

'I know what Sammael did,' said Lucifer. 'There will be consequences, I'm sure. She almost sundered creation with that little stunt.'

'She was angry,' said Jonathan. 'You can understand that, can't you?'

Lucifer's gaze softened and he placed a hand on Jonathan's shoulder. 'Yes,' he said. 'That I can understand very well.'

They walked over to where Sammael, Savantha, Elgar and Cay sat huddled. They looked at Lucifer and he looked at them. Nobody said anything until Savantha held out her maimed hands to show him what Baal had done. Appalled at her injuries, Lucifer bowed his head.

'I . . . I'm . . . sorry,' he said.

'Well, there's something I never thought I'd hear,' said Elgar. 'Can we go home now? It's been a testing day.'

'Yes,' said Lucifer, smiling at the cat. 'You can go home now.'

Ignatius raised himself from his pillows, woken from a strange dream by the happy singing of the village at the back of his mind. A smile drew itself across the vicar's weary face and he lay back, chuckling to himself, his damaged heart beating strongly inside his bruised chest.

'Oh, my bonny lad,' he whispered to the early-evening sky outside his window. 'Well done. So very well done!' Leaping out of bed, he shrugged on his dressing gown and thundered down the stairs. '*Grimm!*' he bellowed. '*Grimm, he's found her! Our boy has found her!*'

He ran outside, told Montgomery and Stubbs and pelted across the green to the pond. Villagers stared in worried amazement as their friend and protector, dressed in pyjamas and with his dressing gown flapping behind him, ran across the green with his arms outstretched, laughter bursting from his lungs.

'*Brass! He's done it, Jonathan's found his mother!*'

The massive dragon opened her eyes and reared up from the

pond, towering over the water. Her lips drew back and she roared triumphantly at the sky. Everyone who hadn't heard Ignatius certainly heard Brass. Dropping whatever they were doing, they hurried to the green, wondering what on earth was happening. They were met with the sight of Ignatius spinning round like a top in his bare feet, and the two gargoyles trying to get him to stop in case he had a seizure.

'Has he gone mad?' asked Stubbs, trying in vain to catch hold of the hem of Ignatius's dressing gown.

'I don't know!' said Montgomery, his expression a mingling of panic and excitement.

Within minutes everyone was there with them. Montgomery and Stubbs danced in happiness on top of Brass's head, their stone feet clanking out a rhythmic tarantella. The dragon just grinned. Music drifted across the village as Mr Flynn put Beethoven's *Ode to Joy* on his old record player and turned the volume up to full. Sweeping up his wife, he danced with her across the grass. Everyone joined in: Grimm, Mr Peters, Professor Morgenstern, Angus McFadden, Clara and Cecily Hayward, Lucia Silkwood. Everyone danced.

And Hobbes End sang as it had never sung before: a melody of pure and simple happiness.

Choosing Sides

J onathan stood by the hedge that surrounded the windmill
and looked out over the village. It had been a week since
Sammael had regained her wings and Hobbes End was once
again at peace – but peace that had come at a price.

Ashamed of what she had done in her rage – aware of the
terrible risk she had taken – Sammael kept to herself and spent
most of her time walking alone in the forest. There was one
thing which helped ease her troubled heart however, and that
was Raphael. Upon returning to Hobbes End, Sammael had
recovered her brother's body from Heaven and laid it to rest in
the churchyard next to that of Gabriel. Raphael Executor was
finally at peace.

Absently rubbing a waxy privet leaf between thumb and forefinger, Jonathan thought about his father. Every time he did so
he felt the familiar squeeze deep inside his chest, but impercep-
tibly the pain was changing. It didn't go away, but it was becoming
something else – something that could eventually be understood
and accepted, regardless of how much the loss hurt. Sammael
had added Darriel's name to the memorial she had built for

Gabriel, and tonight the whole village would be with Jonathan and Savantha when they said their goodbyes at a service that Ignatius had organised.

In the days that had followed his return, Jonathan had watched as a putty-covered Grimm fixed every broken window in the village. He smiled as he thought how gentle and attentive the big man had been towards Savantha. She'd been tucked up in the guest room of the vicarage – next door to Jonathan – and the awful wounds in her hands were stitched and bandaged. Under Grimm's tender care Savantha had rapidly regained her strength, and when she wasn't walking with Jonathan she was often in Grimm's company. Once her hands had fully healed, Grimm had promised to teach her how to play the piano.

Jonathan had also been hugely relieved when a stethoscope-wielding Grimm had pronounced Ignatius's heart fully recovered from Baal's attack, and once again the vicar walked the bounds of his parish, clad in tweeds and chewing on his unlit pipe. Jonathan often accompanied Ignatius on his walks. They didn't talk much to each other – they didn't need to.

Jonathan turned round and looked at Sammael and Lucifer as they sat on the grass next to the windmill, hunched over a chessboard they had borrowed from Ignatius's study. They hadn't said a word for hours. Jonathan thought about what Lucifer had said to him about there being consequences to Sammael's actions. Would the damage she'd caused to reality end up being something they'd regret? He shivered and tried not to dwell on it.

'You're thinking again,' said Cay, coming to stand next to him. She was wearing a new T-shirt with the words *Stupid Magnificent* printed on it, a gift from her parents.

'Are you finally being allowed out of your mum's sight without an armed guard?' he asked her.

She smiled at him. 'Almost.'

'How are you feeling? You got some nasty cuts in Hell.'

'One of the benefits of being a werewolf is that you're difficult to kill,' said Cay. 'In a couple more days even the scars will have faded.'

'I'm glad,' said Jonathan. He paused a moment. 'Thank you,' he added.

'What for?'

'Everything,' He put an arm around her shoulders and gave her a squeeze. '*Meine kleine rote Wölfin.*'

'Yeah, yeah,' she said, playfully thumping him in the chest, but unable to hide her happiness at having saved them from Baal.

'Greetings!' said Elgar, jumping up to balance precariously on top of the hedge.

'Hey, cat,' said Jonathan, reaching out to scratch Elgar behind the ears.

'You know what?' said Elgar.

'What?'

'That a hungry cat must be in search of an open fridge. I'm starving. Shall we go and deprive Grimm of some ice cream while his back's turned?'

Jonathan smiled, Cay smiled, and together with Elgar they walked across the village green in search of mischief.

'I rather like those three,' said Lucifer, grinning over the top of his cup of tea.

'Aren't you full of surprises,' replied Sammael.

Lucifer nodded, moving his bishop to threaten Sammael's queen. 'It would have been . . . interesting if Belial had managed to steal the real Gabriel's Clock and break into Heaven,' he observed.

'How so?' asked Sammael, moving her rook to stave off Lucifer's attack.

'Well, Belial wouldn't have known it, but he and whatever demons he had with him would have ended up in a ruined city, fighting another archdemon that looked like an angel. Rather ironic, don't you think?'

'And how would we have freed the souls of the angels trapped inside if Baal and Belial had wiped each other out?'

Lucifer looked thoughtful for a moment. 'Yes, good point. Still, we'll never know now, will we?' He moved his knight to once again put Sammael on the defensive.

'Why did you help us?' the angel asked, not taking her eyes from the chessboard.

An expression of profound regret appeared on Lucifer's face, then vanished just as quickly. 'It's difficult to explain,' he said. 'I've been telling myself I didn't care about creation, but you know that's not true. You knew that the moment I let you beat me at Armageddon.'

Sammael looked at him and nodded.

'And I could sense that something was terribly wrong with Raphael, but still I chose not to intervene.'

'Don't forget you saved many of the Seraphim,' said Sammael. 'That news alone filled me with so much joy.'

'It was too little, too late,' said Lucifer. 'I stood in the wreckage of Heaven, looking at the results of my pride, and I realised that it was time to make a stand. I know creation will never forgive me for what I have done, for all the damage I have caused, but I decided to help anyway. It was Darriel that hammered the point home.'

'Jonathan's father? You saw him?'

'Yes. I felt something happening to Heaven's gates and I arrived just in time to meet Darriel before his soul moved on. He made his feelings on what I should do very clear. After he left I stood there alone for quite some time, but I kept coming back to the same thing.'

'Which is?'

'Jonathan. The more I ponder the impossibility of his existence the more I realise that not only does creation want him to exist, it *needs* him to exist. We are dinosaurs, Sammael, you and I. We belong to a different age, but Jonathan, he is here for a reason. I don't know what it is yet, but it must be important – and so I did what I could to help, however little and however late.'

Sammael smiled and nodded. 'Your intervention was quite timely.'

'It was,' said Lucifer, 'but not soon enough to stop you going too far. You realise that not allowing Baal's soul to go back to the heart of creation – then ripping a hole in the fabric of reality so you could send him off to eternal torment – may well come back to haunt you. Haunt us?'

It was Sammael's turn to look sad. 'I know,' she said. 'I was just so angry.'

'That I can understand,' said Lucifer. 'Still, I have a feeling that we're going to need each other's help at some point. There's one archdemon left and she's been very quiet for a very long time.'

'You mean Lilith?'

'Yes, Lilith. She's far more intelligent than either Belial or Baal, and I think she knows that you didn't beat me on the battlefield that day.'

'Well, we'll deal with her if the need arises,' said Sammael. 'There's no need to go looking for monsters under the bed, is there?'

'No,' said Lucifer, moving one last chess piece. 'Check, I think.'

Sammael smiled and moved her queen. 'Sorry to disappoint you, but checkmate, I think!'

Lucifer scowled.

'And don't you dare say you let me win,' said Sammael.

'Now would I?' replied Lucifer, feigning a wounded look.

Sammael cleared the chessboard. 'Another game?'

Lucifer nodded and Sammael held out two fists, a different-coloured chess piece in each one.

'Black or white?' she asked.

Lucifer gave her a mischievous smile, and chose.

Epilogue

Cutting Edge

Michael's legendary spear hung in the gap between worlds. Two metres in length, its black-glass haft was pitted and scored by a terrible explosion. The narrow blade remained sharp though, sharp enough to cut a slice from the solar winds, sharp enough to cut a slice from just about anything.

Grasped for the first time in centuries, the weapon stopped its eternal spinning and woke.

Lilith allowed herself a brief, chilling smile as she studied her prize. 'We have such great work to do, you and I,' she whispered to the weapon, kissing the blade, claiming it as her own. 'No more games. It's time to undo this flawed universe of Lucifer's. Sammael has wounded creation and I shall use this blade to end its suffering. The only question is . . . where to make the first incision?'

Author's Note

I t may interest readers to know that Elgar is constantly frustrated by his lack of opposable thumbs. He's been that way since I first imagined him – a slightly mad cat, bouncing about on the keyboard of the vicarage piano, trying to hammer out his version of chopsticks with all four paws.

There is indeed an M. R. James ghost story called 'Oh, Whistle, and I'll Come to You, My Lad', written in Cambridge in 1903. Who is to say he didn't get the idea from an angel's description of Hell?

I named Raphael's wife Bethesda after the fountain at the heart of Central Park in New York. The fountain is topped by a beautiful statue called *Angel of Waters*, designed by Emma Stebbins in 1873. The word Bethesda means *house of mercy* in Aramaic, and relates to a pool of water in the Muslim quarter of Jerusalem. Legend has it that an angel would occasionally stir the waters of the pool and heal the first person to enter it of any sickness they might have.

Before his final battle, Baal sings the traditional English folk song, 'Greensleeves'. It is not known who wrote the song, but it is likely to be Elizabethan in origin.

When Sammael destroys Baal, she quotes from the sonnet 'Ozymandias' by Percy Bysshe Shelley, first published in 1818 in the *Examiner*.

The inscription on Gabriel's headstone quotes from the poem 'High Flight', written by Pilot Officer John Gillespie Magee Jr on 18 August 1941.

Hilton Pashley
Norwich, November 2014

GABRIEL'S CLOCK

HILTON PASHLEY

Jonathan is the only half-angel, half-demon in the universe, and now the forces of Hell want him for their own purpose.

Aided by a vicar with a broken heart, a big man with a cricket bat and a very rude cat, Jonathan races to find the mysterious Gabriel's Clock. If he doesn't find it then his family and friends will die, but, if he does, then he risks starting a war between Heaven and Hell that could engulf them all.

Gabriel's clock is ticking . . . and time is running out.

9781783441136 £6.99

THE PIPER

DANNY WESTON

He who pays the piper calls the tune

On the eve of World War Two, Peter and Daisy are
evacuated to a remote farmhouse. From the moment
they arrive, they are aware that something evil haunts
the place. Who plays the eerie music that can only be
heard at night? And why is Daisy so irresistibly drawn
to it? When Peter uncovers a dark family secret, he
begins to realise that his sister is in terrible danger,
and to save her he must face an
ancient curse…

'Wonderfully twisty chiller
that's sure to make you want
to keep all of the lights on'
Scotsman

9781783440511   £6.99

THE DOGS

ALLAN STRATTON

Cameron and his mom have been on the run for five
years. His father is hunting them. At least, that's what
Cameron's been told. When they settle in an isolated
farmhouse, Cameron starts to see and hear things that
aren't possible. Soon he's questioning everything he
thought he knew – and his own mind.

Something is waiting for him, something from long
ago. Cameron must uncover its dark secrets before it
tears him apart.

'Brilliant, page-turning and eerie.
Had me guessing to the very end'
Joseph Delaney

'Creepy, satisfying and exciting'
Bookseller

9781783442256 £7.99